Words Left Unspoken

Brionna Carter

Contents

Chapter 1

N O. 1 ;   A LETTER TO YOUR BEST FRIEND

FEBRUARY 27th, 2013

Dear Somebody,

You know I would have started this letter off with 'dear -insert name here-' but I wanted to write this letter to my best friend and the thought struck me that I don't have a best friend. Yes, I have friends, lots of friends, I'm not saying I'm popular or well-known, it's just I do have quite a few mates. But I realised that I don't have that one best friend. You know, the one you've known all your life, the one who you share your hopes and fears and secrets, the one you trust with your life. I don't have that.

Never did. Probably never will. I guess I just don't do best friends any way. I can't seem to allow myself to be that close to another person. Distance is a good thing for me.

So, I'm going to address this letter to the person who has come closest to being my best friend. And that's you Georgia.

You know where I am right now? I'm sat in our favourite café, the small little coffee shop in the corner of Fairbank Road. I'm sat right in the back, where the lights are low and the music is a mere hum. We used to come here every Friday afterschool, it's still my favourite place in the city. The memories are stronger here than anywhere else, I can smell, taste, touch all the times we sat here, just chatting and laughing whatever mundane matter that came up in our lives. I miss those times, Georgia. I don't know where time has gone, but I know it took you with it.

We didn't really start talking until, what, Year 9? Yeah, Year 9. Back then we were in different friendship groups and it wasn't until Lucy went on holiday and left you by yourself that we started hanging out.

You were quiet and shy with a kind smile and warm brown eyes and I was brash and loud and dirty-minded. And you always say that I polluted your mind. That before me, you were innocent and practically ignorant to the atrocities of the world. And then I opened your eyes, I slowly eased you into the world of crude jokes and cynicism.

As the years went by and we grew older, the jokes and brashness that was first nature for me, became second nature to you, but you were still shy. Even now, you still have that hesitancy you had when we first met.

You're an introvert.

To others you're quiet and timid and smiling but it's only when you're around me, around people you're comfortable with that you come out of your shell and you show just how brilliant you are. You know, you were favourite person when we were in secondary school? Even though you're three days younger than me (you always insisted that you would have been two weeks older if you hadn't had arrived late), I sort of looked up to you (literally, you're five foot nine). Cause you were one of the few people I was truly comfortable around.

You didn't remind me of my insecurities and my inadequacy at practically everything. We had the same flaws you and I. We silently acknowledged them and saluted ourselves for them. Well, perfection is overrated isn't it? Imperfection is underrated and you and I were way past imperfect.

You know, I thought (I still do) think you're the funniest and most genuine person I had ever met.

Some days, you would piss me off. You would piss me off so much I would wish I never knew you, but when I next saw you the anger would instantly vanish and I couldn't for the life of me remember why I was angry with you. You were the only person who could get away with that kind of murder, Georgia. Others would have been ten feet in the ground but you were always ten feet higher.

I remember sometime near the end of Year 9 (when you and I were officially friends and you were finally getting used to my dirty jokes) that a new girl came into our year. Christine Wellington. She was from London and everybody just fell in love with her. Mainly because of her accent and her glossy hair and perfect fashion sense.

She hung with the 'cool crowd' but when she wasn't with them, she was always with you and I remember. I remember that day when I walked into History and I saw her talking to you. And you seemed so close and you were laughing, Georgia. You were laughing in that way you and I would laugh at a private joke and I felt this irrational wave of jealousy strike me. And a small resentment for the London girl bedded inside my chest because I had a stupid fear she would take you away from me. Why wouldn't she?

You were the only person in that room worth talking to. I just stared for God knows how long, debating on what to do and then I noticed she was going to sit in my seat. My seat.

Where I always sat next you and I quickly snapped out of my stupor and told her exactly that. It was my seat. Not hers. Not anyone else's. And I stomped over and sat down. I took my rightful place beside you. I'm petty that way you see.

I'm possessive with the things, the people I love but it's a silent, controlled kind of possessive because I don't want to seem clingy. Back then I felt this intense need to keep you by my side no matter what. It's still there and I doubt it will ever leave.

Georgia, do you remember in Year 11 when we were lounging about in the English corridor with our other mates and the two of us were joking around, at what I can't even remember now and Emma looked at us. She smiled fondly and said, "you two are best friends aren't you?"

And I don't know. I just felt this knot in my stomach because. ...because I've never had a best friend and you were the closest thing to it. I was conflicted for a second, I didn't know whether to say yes or no. Because you were but at the same time you weren't.

But I didn't say anything you see. Neither of us said anything to that, we just remained quiet, a long silence stretching over us. And I tried not to feel disappointed when you shrugged and changed the subject. I really did.

And I guess that's why I keep saying that you were closest thing I've ever had to a best mate. We never called each other best friends. Because after, Christine Wellington finally backed off and got the message that you were mine, you had made another new friend.

Zoe Cooper. Zoe, who you adored and constantly talked about and I would hate myself for the jealousy I felt when you were with her. It's pathetic. You never belonged to me. It's pathetic and stupid but I always had a problem when it came to sharing you.

You and I were the closest in our group of friends and no one else seemed to reach that level of familiarity we were with each other. No one else except Zoe. You were my closest friend but I think you were closer to Zoe than you were with me.

Best friends trust each other completely, they share their fears and hopes and dreams and their secrets. I trusted you, and even though you would joke about not trusting me with a pen, I know you did.

You know what I loved about us? There was always that one tether connecting us. It was our disbelief in the world to meet our expectations and the disbelief in ourselves to meet the world's expectations. I never found that in anyone else. That mutual and underlying cynicism in so many things. We never shared our deepest fears. I never told you my darkest secrets in fear of repulsing you and sending you running. I couldn't have that. I needed you by my side.

So I kept them tucked away, folded and hidden in the dark and I would tell you of my shallow fears. Never in a serious manner, always jokingly, always to make you laugh. We loved to joke you and I, our impeccable humour connected us and kept us strong but it also kept us apart. There was always this wall between us, Georgia. This wall I was too scared to pass. This wall I didn't know how to pass.

You know, in all the time that we've known each other, I've only seen you cry once. And that once was enough because it was like something icy and heavy had smacked me straight in my gut. And I guess that's why I tried so hard to keep you smiling, to keep you happy because I couldn't handle you when you were sad, I couldn't handle myself when you were sad.

That's thing about us. We always skimmed the surface when came to the real issues, to the emotions. We never delved deeper and even now, I feel that there was a side to you, a softer, more emotive side that I was never brave enough to meet. And it's the same with you.

There's the emotional, and doubtful and insecure side to me that you never quite knew, you saw glimpses and snapshots but that was it. We kept our vulnerable sides leashed and out of sight. If we had ventured to know every aspect of each other, if we were brave enough and less childish, and stopped hiding behind our jokes and immaturity I think. I think we could have had the deeper sense of friendship we both craved from one another.

Love, Morgana

CHAPTER 2

NO. 2 ; A LETTER TO YOUR CRUSH

DECEMBER 2nd, 2013

Dear James,

James. James. James. James.

It's thanks to you that I like that name so much. I'm infatuated with it. Despite what others say, it's not at all boring. It's the epitome of elegance and class. I like how it sounds on my tongue, how easily it rolls off, leaving behind a slight shudder. It suits you and I simply can't imagine you with another name.

James Baxter. There, I wrote your full name. I might as well, nobody else but me is going to see these letters. No one ever will because I fully intend on either ;

a) burning these letters to ground.

b) burying them deep in the earth.

Or c) locking them away, far away.

You probably already know this, word travels fast in our school but I like you. There. I said it, well wrote it, I fancy the pants off you James Baxter and I wish I had the balls to tell you in person.

Now, James, here's a question I've been asking myself for God's know how long. Why you? Why do I like you? I mean, there are much cuter guys (not that I stand a chance with any of them, but still) and I just don't understand why it has to be you. Can I just say, you can be a right prick to me? Just last week you punched me in the shoulder because I apparently tried to copy one of your answers. (I was just stretching my arms, with no intention of doing such a thing) And how about yesterday when you shoved me so hard I nearly fell. Admittedly, you did catch me before I hit the ground, but still.

To be honest, I am a prick to you too. I punch you and insult you but that's only because I like you so much. And I could just laugh at how juvenile my crush on you is and I could laugh until I die at how immature my handling of it is. It's just a crush. Nothing more. It'll pass like all the others but here's the problem. I don't want it too. I like how you make me feel James. I like the butterflies and the quickening heartbeats. I like having your name, your face, your voice running around in my head, all day, every day. I love that you occupy my thoughts because if you didn't something darker and twisted would be plaguing my mind.

I'll never tell you this. I'd sooner jump off a cliff than admit this to you but…you have nice eyes. They're coloured a light olive green that turns gold in the sunlight and its honestly breathtaking. You don't have the best eyes in our year.

That award goes to Kyle Witter with his bright blue eyes, but he's a dick and he pisses me off. But your eyes are my favourite. And your stupid messy blonde hair. Don't you own a comb? Most of the boys' hair are neat and brushed but yours is always in disarray and I always want to run my hands through it.

I almost did.

A few weeks ago in Biology when we were partnered up and you were tying your apron, your hair was falling in your eyes and I had this sudden urge to push it back and rake my hands through that blonde mess of hair. I nearly did you know, my hand was just a few inches from your head when you suddenly looked up and I had to quickly withdraw my hand. I had to make it look like I was swatting a fly away and you just watched, slightly bemused.

You patted my arm (like I was one of your mates) and you made some stupid joke about my incompetence and I didn't know whether to kick you or kiss you (always the latter).

Really I'm wasting my time with you because you don't feel the same way. You treat me more like an annoying brother (I would say sister but that would mean you see me as a girl) than a potential girlfriend. But then there are times, those rare moments when it's just the two of us and you get this look on your face. Like you're seeing me for the first time, like you're see more to me. Your eyes. Have I mentioned how much I love your eyes in those moments?

They're a bright, almost luminescent green that remind me of the way sunlight filters through the leaves. Impossibly green and so full of life. Sometimes (oh so rarely), you reach out and touch my hair or my shoulder ever so gently and my breathing will stop and my insides will be squirming under the pressure of your gaze. But that look only lasts mere seconds before you snap out of it and return to the matter hand, and I'm left there flailing and shocked and feeling as if I imagined it all.

You're a frustrating boy, James but I never try to imagine or even delude myself for a second that I stand a chance with you. Because well, you're you and I'm me. I don't think I'll be enough for you. I haven't much to offer. You would be sorely disappointed.

I remember the day we met. It was the beginning of our first year in sixth form and it was the first English lesson of the year. Ms. Kiplin wanted us to be "familiar" with each other, so she gave us some name tags and made us go around the class and introduce ourselves. Which was stupid and pointless by the way, because nobody on such a dreary day could be bothered. I was laughing at Georgia's name tag (I can't even remember what she put now, something hilarious though) and I sort of bumped into you (okay, crashed).

I immediately apologised, spluttering like the idiot I was. You didn't look annoyed, you looked...amused. You were one of the new students, as I had never seen you before and believe me, I would have remembered a face as handsome as yours. I'm not good with boys, like at all, they make me nervous and self-conscious and I would have walked away, blushing and mumbling apologies if you hadn't been smiling at me like that. Like what I don't know but I liked it, it calmed me down.

"James," you said.

"James," I repeated it only because I liked the sound of it, the way it felt in my mouth.

You thought I was a little weird then, I could tell from the curious way you were looking at me, but you didn't comment on it. You just nodded. Your eyes flitted down to my name tag and you cocked an eyebrow, "Motherfucker Jones?"

I was confused for a few seconds and then I remembered and laughed. I shook my head, "No, no, uhm, it's from the movie Horrible Bosses, have you seen it?"

I was trying to act cool you see, and not seem at all affected by your striking eyes. I was failing. Terribly.

I saw the corners of your lips tug upwards as you sat down on the edge of the table, "No, I haven't. What's your real name, then?"

"M-Morgana, Morgana," I replied.

My eyes were roaming all over your face, taking in your messy brown hair, your pink lips that were pulled up in a smile, your defined jawline and finally your olive green eyes. I would officially, from the bottom of my heart like to compliment you on your face, James. You have a gorgeous face.

"Morgana," you repeated in turn. I blinked, surprised. My name sounded soft and warm, and almost like a melody when it came out of your mouth. When others said it, it was hard and clunky and awkward, but from your tongue I didn't hate my name so much.

I don't know why I said yes. I sounded like an arsehole.

"Pleasure to meet you, Morgana," you said, your smile broadening and I let myself stare for a few moments. When you smile at a girl like that James, like they're the sun and the very air you need, you really shouldn't be surprised when the girl starts falling for you.

English Lit has become my favourite lesson. Not the subject itself. Not the teacher. Not the people. Just you. Along with Biology, it's the only class we have together and every Monday and Thursday, I am buzzing with nerves and excitement for the lesson because you're in it.

The days that you aren't are severely disappointing. I'll walk into the class and my eyes will instantly find you. You'll be sat in the second row, sharing a table with Kyle Witter. I sit in the table in front of you and every five minutes I make up an excuse (any excuse) to turn around talk to you. And you feign annoyance, but you'll talk to me and we'll joke for a few seconds before Miss tells me to face the front.

We're friends, you and I aren't we? I mean, we squabble over pointless things but we're friends. I know your friendship is all you can offer me, all you have to offer me, but I can't help but wish for more. It scares me though.

These feelings. I've had crushes before, but they've been fleeting and meaningless but this one is different. It's deeper, it's seeded firmly in my chest and grows and grows and refuses to leave. It scares me. I think if you ever recuperated my feelings for you, a part of me would be jumping for joy, but an even bigger part of me would be terrified and running for the hills. You want to know why?

Because I don't think I deserve you. You deserve someone like Sera Hasan, the Iranian beauty who everyone is after, or Imogen Collins, pretty, petite Imogen Collins. You're funny and cute and kind and clever and everything I want wrapped up in one and I don't deserve you. Which is why, the bitter pill of inevitable rejection from you will be easier to swallow.

You'll find a girl, who isn't a bumbling mess of self-hatred and dark thoughts hiding behind bright smiles and crude jokes, you'll find the perfect girl for you who deserves your blinding grins, your kind touches and sweet words. And the realisation that that girl isn't me, will never be me, really stings.

Love, Morgana

CHAPTER 3

NO. 3 ; A LETTER TO YOUR FATHER

DECEMBER 5th, 2013

Dear Dad,

When Mum passed away she took a large chunk of you with her. For the first few weeks all you did was lay in bed, you covered yourself in Mum's clothes and sprayed the room with her favourite perfume. Every time I passed your room, I would hear Mum's records playing, and every time it was like a punch in the gut.

Mum's sister took care of us for those weeks, took us to school, made us dinner, gave us a shoulder to cry on. She said that you weren't yourself right now and you needed some time to come to terms with Mum's death.

Eight months.

That's how long you stayed immobile in your bed, you were fired from your job and diagnosed with depression. It was the worst state I had ever seen you in and it broke my heart. Everything about you was just grey and everywhere you went you drained the colour and life. And for a while, I was scared I was going to lose you too. And I cried myself to sleep almost every night.

Don't you realise you have three daughters who were as deeply affected and devastated by her death? Don't you realise that we needed you?

It was a little over three years after Mum's death, I was around thirteen and I remember that particular November morning, I had woken up, pulled on my school uniform and gone downstairs for breakfast. I had been pouring myself some milk when a tall, dark-skinned woman dressed in a pink robe came waltzing into the kitchen.

She instantly froze and smiling sheepishly at me, she said, "Oh, uh, good morning."

It was then, Dad, that you came into the room. You placed an arm around her waist and smiled. "Morgana, meet my friend Jasmin, Jasmin meet my daughter, Morgana."

Friend. Huh. Jasmin's smile widened into a bright grin as she stepped forward and offered her hand to me, "Hi, it's lovely to finally meet you."

I blinked. I just stared at her, finding it hard to process the situation. Jasmin glanced worriedly back at you when I didn't do or say anything for several seconds.

You frowned at me, "Morgana, say hello."

In that moment I wanted more than anything to throw the bowl of cereal in your face. I shook my head and angrily stormed out of the kitchen. I couldn't believe it. You brought another woman, a complete stranger to our house without a care about us.

Did you think I would welcome her? Did you think I would be happy to see some strange woman in my house? Jesus Christ, for years all you did was stay in your room, for years after Mum's death you were a blank slate and then one day you just brought some random woman.

I was so angry with you, for the rest of day I was fuming, I didn't pay attention in class and I ended up in a pretty bad fight with one of the kids. Ariel said, we should be happy that you found someone and I didn't speak to her for weeks. What about Mum? You couldn't just replace her with some random woman.

Despite my protests (I was pretty loud about my opinions), Jasmin came round more often, and before I knew it she had moved in, and next thing I knew, after two and a half years together, you married her.

I want you to know that as much as I was against you marrying her, I want you to know that I don't hate her. I mean, at first I did but now, I realise Ariel was right. She does make you happy, you got a new job, and you're smiling and laughing more often now. And if Jasmin can lift you from the darkness that had engulfed for some many years, then I can't fault her.

Dad, you know I love you right? I don't show it and I don't act like it but I do. I love you. I try to be a good daughter. I try to smile and be the best that I can but 'the best' isn't in me. Nothing is. There's a hole where my heart should be, a big gaping chasm that sucks in any affection or love. I try to fill it with food, with laughter and jokes and false optimism but nothing works.

I haven't achieved or done anything noteworthy. I'm not smart. I'm not talented. I'm not beautiful but I'm not ugly. My grades are mediocre. Everything I do, I am is mediocre and I just don't understand how you can stand to be around me.

You realise that you don't know me, right? You don't know the simple things about me. My favourite colour, my favourite movie, my career plans, none of that. Yes, you know the general things like my grades and allergies but it's the small, seemingly unimportant things that turn out to be the most cherished.

I just. I wish you could tell me I was good enough. I wish you could tell me, that what I am, what I do is enough. You never did. You always saved the praise for others. You were always there for the others but never for me. Hell, the dog got more attention than me. The dog. And that mongrel shits everywhere.

Being the middle child of three girls is no good. There are absolutely no perks. You are hardly noticed. The attention is always on the eldest and the youngest and the middle child is left to fend for themselves.

Jasmin, tell me, because I know you're more truthful than Dad, tell me, I'm not the favourite child am I? I'm not.

A few months ago, during one of our arguments, Evelyn revealed that I wasn't. Evelyn is the favourite, then Ariel and then me. Whatever. It's okay. I don't mind. I like it. I don't think I could stand it if Ariel or Evelyn were your least favourites. I'm glad it's me. It's freeing, knowing that your expectations of me are so low they are barely even there. It means I don't have to stress myself out to please you. Because I'm done. Trying to please you that is. I used to crave your praise when I was younger, I used to live of it but now I'm older and wiser and filled with so much indifference for the world, I find that I no longer care for your expectations. You have Evelyn and Ariel for that. You don't need me.

Green. That's my favourite colour by the way. Green.

My favourite film is American Beauty and as for my career plans? No idea.

Love, Morgana.

CHAPTER 4

NO.4 ; A LETTER TO YOUR SIBLING

DECEMBER 19th, 2013

Dear Evelyn,

You've always been so perfect. You've always been so loved. Evelyn Jones. The Queen of Burbank School. I've always thought of you as the 'better' version of me.

The older, prettier, funnier and more loved version. Because, come on, with a name as beautiful Evelyn Jones and a face as beautiful yours, who wouldn't fall in love with you? You're only a year older than me and yet you act as if you're in your twenties. You treat me like I'm a three-year-old who doesn't understand anything.

When I first started in Year Seven at Burbank, I was really excited. I was so hyped because I'd finally left primary school and I was in secondary school. I'd heard tales of what happened there. I'd seen the movies, I'd read the books. You grow breasts, make friends, meet boys, fall in love, get a boyfriend, go to parties, etc. Secondary school is apparently supposed to the best times of your life.

God. I hope that's not true.

If I'm being honest, secondary school was mediocre at best. Sure, I did friends, I did meet boys but the partying and the dating bit? Didn't happen for me. As you know (you made comments about it to your mates) I spent my evenings and weekends, locked in my room either reading (The Hunger Games, whoop-whoop), on YouTube, or surfing Tumblr.

Whilst you, oh dear sister, spent your free time going out, either partying, making out with your boyfriends (yes, plural) or bitching about someone who was supposedly your friend. At times you would come back home at one in the morning, dirty and completely wasted and I would hide you, make sure neither Dad nor Jasmin saw you in such a drunken state. Every time, I held your hair as you puked in the toilet. Every time I cleaned you up. Every time I hugged you as cried over whichever boy had broken your heart. And the next day, you would act like you didn't remember or didn't care about it.

From Year Seven to Year Ten, I was referred to as Evelyn's Sister. It was only in Year Eleven when I nearly burnt down one of the Food Tech rooms that I got a new moniker. I was The Girl Who Nearly Burnt the School Down. Which is so much better, much more freeing than being called Evelyn's Sister'. From then on, my connection to you was only by blood and the passing glances we gave each other in the corridors on our way to our next class.

It's another Friday night and I'm in my bedroom as I write this. Guess where you are? That's right, you're at Christine Wellington's Christmas party. Everybody, who is anybody in sixth form is at her party. Good to know that I fit in the 'nobody' category. I swear if you come back at some Godforsaken hour, drunk out of your mind

I will not help you. I will just leave you there, and let Jasmin or Dad see what their perfect Evelyn is up to.

You know, you're not as perfect and as collected as everybody thinks you are. Deep down, you are as ugly and twisted as me. You and I, we've had our fair share of fights over these years, show me siblings who don't fight and I'll give you a million pounds.There was this one fight, the fight that started from something trivial, the fight that cut the deepest.

About three months ago, you and I got into argument. I was sitting in the living room, reading an article on the Guardian about the latest Captain America film, when you stormed in, demanding that I give you the money I owed you because you were going out with your latest boyfriend.

"I can't," I told you, "I'm skint."

"It's been two months, Morgana," you frowned, "I want my money, I need it to buy a new top."

"You have lots of tops."

"Yes but I'm seeing Sean later and none of them go with my jeans."

"Fine," I said, "Borrow one of mine."

You scoffed, "And end up looking like a drag queen?"

And from there, the fight quickly escalated. Lots of threats were given and lots of insults were thrown but none hurt, none of them stung as much as the way you looked at me when you said, "No wonder you're nobody's favourite."

"What?"

Your smile was derisive and colder than the arctic. "Didn't you guess? You're not Dad's favourite child, I am and Ariel is Jasmin's fave."

I felt my hands curl and clench into tight fists.

"You're just the third wheel," you sneered, "They tolerate you. Have you noticed that Dad wasn't even surprised when you got that D in Biology? That's because he's learnt to set his expectations low when it comes to you."

I swallowed. "Shut up."

"Why?" You sneered, "I'm only telling you truth. You're the third wheel. The odd one out."

"Get the hell away from me, Evelyn."

"Gladly and you know what? Keep the damn money, you need it more than I do."

With that you turned and left the room, leaving me there, feeling empty and suddenly so self-aware of everything that was wrong with me. Right then, I hated the very skin I was in, I hated the sound of my breathing, I hated, hated, absolutely loathed the tears that stung my eyes and I wanted nothing more than to curl into a ball and disappear from the world.

Evelyn, there are two distinct sides to you. The smiles and the sneers. You can smile and listen to others troubles, you always try your best to be there for those who need you, you're confident and intelligent and you stick with those you love through the stormiest of days.

Oh, but you can also be so cruel, you can be so mindless in your endeavour to hurt, to inflict pain that you aim all your pistols at the person's weakest points. You're kind but vindictive by nature.

You are only as good as the world allows you to be.

You know how to get into someone's skin, you know what to say to dismantle every wall they put up, and you know just how worthless and so fuelled with self-hatred you can make people feel. You very rarely let your darker side out. You pent up all your rage and unleash it in private moments where no one can judge you. You usually unleash that side on me and over the years I've learnt to build up walls strong enough to keep your toxic words out.There are times, Evelyn, there are times where I absolutely DESPISE you. There are times where I wish with all my heart that you never existed.Those are usually times where you push me too far and I crumble. Most of the time, though, do you know what I feel towards you?

It's not jealousy as you'd expect. No, I don't want your life or your friends or your looks. No, I feel sorry for you. The reason Dad loves you so much, the reason he is so devoted and pays the most attention to you is because you are the exact replica of Mum when she was your age. You remind him of her and he gains a strange comfort from that.

Here's the cold, hard truth my dear sister. You resemble Mum in appearance but not in spirit.You are not as compassionate, you are not as forgiving, you are not as loving or as loyal as she was.

I feel sorry for you because you are constantly compared to her and you know that you will never be able to be as inspiring as she was. You know you are nothing compared to her. And you can run away from that truth Evelyn, you can hide from it behind your lipgloss smile and raving popularity, but it is truth and the truth remains. I feel sorry for you. Jasmin, Dad, Ariel and oh so many people's expectations of you are so high and so heavy that you're buckling under the weight of it all.

What's sad is that you're living the life of a fictionalised version of yourself. You present this image of a golden girl, the Queen of Burbank School, the most beloved of our family and you think that if you keep batting your eyelids and you keep smiling that nobody will see through that façade but you're wrong. I have. I know what you are.

You are lost.

You have no idea who are you. You have fallen for your own illusion and that's sad, Evelyn. That's really sad. I can admit that I don't know who I am. I can't even begin to try and define myself but you want to know the difference between you and I?

I know I'm lost and I'm searching and God's knows when I'll find myself but the important part is that I am looking. You're lost and you have no idea just how deep in the labyrinth of lies and illusions you are. I hope one day you realise this and I hope it doesn't break you as badly as it did for me.

Love, Morgana.

Chapter 5

Dear Whoever,

Well, I'm not really sure how to start this letter. Like a lot of people, I have a lot of hopes and I have a lot dreams. Over the years some have died and new ones have been born in their place. I don't have a specific career in my mind but I do know I want to do something in psychology or history. Do you want to know my wildest dream?

That one day, I will be somebody. That when I die I will not be forgotten, that my name will go down in the history books. For the seventeen years I've been on this planet, I have not accomplished anything noteworthy, for the seventeen years I have always been the nobody in the sea of somebodies. Sometimes, when I'm particularly bored my mind will stray and I'll imagine what they'll say about me in the history books.

Or something like that. It puts a smile onto my face to think that I could achieve something great, something on par with Cleopatra and William Shakespeare and Martin Luther King Jr. but after a few seconds it depresses me because I know I can never achieve something as brilliant as that. You see, after Mum died, all I could think about was ridding the world of the disease that killed her. Cancer is a sneaky litte thing, its devious and cruel and doesn't care about who it hits.

I dream that I've found the cure for it. It's part of the reason I took Biology as an A Level, the other part is because, well, Biology is interesting. I like knowing how things work. When I was a kid, I liked taking clocks apart, analysing each component, studying the mechanisms. I used to marvel at how everything little thing connected. I spent my childhood taking clocks apart. Evelyn thought I was really for doing that and my dad used to get really cross when he found I'd taken apart another one of his watches.

Whilst most people would concentrate on the Why, I would always focus on the How. How does it work? How does this happen? Because once you understand the How, you can understand the Why. My brain is wired that way. Nowadays, I don't take clocks apart anymore, I know the mechanisms of a clock like I know the back of my hand. I know how a clock ticks, and I know why it ticks. You see the How seeks to understand, it has a genuine curiosity, but the Why, is accusatory and bewildered.

I have a lot of hopes.

I hope that I become somebody.

I hope that I'm imagining the way James Baxter looks at Natalie Huxham, I hope to the stars and beyond he looks at me like that one day.

I hope I feel good enough one day.

I hope Ariel gets that part in the school play she's been wanting for ages.

I hope that I don't fail my upcoming exams.

I hope one day I'll be strong enough.

I hope I find that light at the end of the tunnel.

I hope that I don't always feel this lost.

Hope.

I'm really starting to hate that word. Hope raises you high, it sets you up for disappoint and lets you fall. Hope is bittersweet. Hope never leaves you, even in your darkest moments, even when you're feeling so isolated and your thoughts are blackened, hope crawls in and settles.

Hope clings to you, it refuses to leave and it doesn't lighten the load. It makes it heavier. Everything amplifies when your hope is shattered and you're left broken and wandering in the dark by yourself. You need to squish, stamp, throw, beat down that hope as hard you can the instant it pops up because hope will only bring you pain.

But that's easier said than done.

So, I'm going to say this.

Don't hope. Hope is for the idle. It's for the starry-eyed, the dreamers. Hope builds falsities out of the harsh reality. Those of us who see the world for what it really is, cruel and random, we need to believe. Belief is stronger than hope because belief drives you further than hope ever will.

Love, Morgana.

CHAPTER 6

N0.6; A LETTER TO A STRANGER

JANUARY 1st, 2014

Dear Somebody,

The other day, no, it must have been two years ago? Yeah, well, something like that. (You see when I say 'the other day', it can be yesterday or ten years ago, it doesn't really matter). I remember that day. I was fifteen and turning sixteen in less than one month. And I had just come from an afterschool revision class for the upcoming exams in summer.

I remember. It was the last day of April and the air smelt of lavenders and was thick with humidity. I walked leisurely with my iPod on and earphones in, listening to the latest songs. It was a particularly hot day so I wore my sunglasses and had taken my school blazer off and rolled up my shirt sleeves.

I didn't want to take the main road as it a) too long and too hot b) there was a couple of stray dogs that liked to hang around that area that scared the hell out of me. And so, I turned a corner and entered the local cemetery. It was a little creepy but it was better than the alternative of being mauled by dogs. With Arctic Monkeys playing, I walked down the cobbled path, my eyes lazily wandering around the graveyard, skipping from headstone to headstone.

And that was when I spotted you.

You were under an oak tree, surrounded by a myriad of gravestones but you were only interested in two. You were kneeling, like your legs had given out. Like they couldn't take the weight of all the troubles you held and you sank. Your eyes were trained on two headstones, they were new, maybe only a couple of months old and made of the finest marble. In your lap, lay a bouquet of sunshine yellow carnations that you were gripping tightly.

And oh your face, I will never forget the expression. It was the expression of a person who wore a mask of bravery for the world, who held onto the last scraps of strength they had with all their being. And it was the expression of someone who let that crack and disintegrate only in the most private moment. You were laying bare all your emotions and every thought you ever kept leashed.

I stopped walking and stood frozen and transfixed. I don't think my heart was beating, all I could hear was the faint rustle of the leaves in the summer wind and the occasional chirp of a bird. I knew you. You wore the same black and red uniform of our school. You were in the year below. I was sure I had seen you around.

Not always but sometimes just a flicker of your dark braids among the chattering populous of Burbank School or a flash of your bright smile and the sound of the laughter you caused. I remember. I remember hearing the whispering rumours of a death. A student had lost her father and younger sister to a fatal car crash. It was then, as I silently watched you kneeling by their graves that I realised that student was you.

And I was suddenly transported back.

I was eleven years old again.

Left hand clutching my father's and right hand clutching Evelyn's. Tears streaming down my face as I watched them lower my mother's coffin into the ground. The pounding sunshine of the early spring was cruel and mocking and I wanted to scream and tell them to stop. Tell them that it was all a mistake and that somehow, my mother was still alive.

I never hid my grief like you did, I never tamed it because I never had to. But you, I realise you had to be strong and hold everything up when everyone else was falling apart. You had to put your grief aside for now and concentrate on those who needed you.

Thirty seconds, a minute, five minutes may have passed as I watched you. It didn't surprise me when you started crying. Not silent or controlled, but loud and unrestrained. It was all the pent up rage and grief and emotions you stored. It flooded out in harsh breaths and I was completely frozen. I was almost going to run over to you and offer you a shoulder to cry on. And give you reassuring falsities about how it would be alright, that tomorrow brought a new day and less pain.

I almost did.

Almost.

But I realised this was your moment, a small, private moment of peace in the chaos that submerged your darkly lit world. And so, with a heavy heart I turned and continued on my way.

I saw you three days later in school. You were smiling, it was a painful one. One you use when your energy is running out. I wanted to ask your name, find out your story. We all have a story to tell, and yours looks to be a dark one.

I am writing this letter in Esterlake Cemetery Park, the same cemetery I saw you in two years ago. I'm sat on a bench, on the small hilltop that overlooks the graveyard. It's eerily silent and the wind carries an icy bite to it.

I am writing this letter to tell you all things I wish I had the bravery to say to you back then. I want you to know that it does get better. The pain of losing those you love is one of, if not the most, painful experiences a person can endure. Death is not fair and it has never claimed to be kind. It's as cold as the deepest winters.

I'll tell you this. Time doesn't heal. It numbs. I won't lie to you. The pain you feel that first instant the dagger pierces into your heart is a pain that will remain for as long as you live. For those lucky few, it can heal but for those of us who refuse to let our loved ones go, the pain only numbs. You learn to live with it because it becomes a part of you.

I stumbled and crashed through the death of my mother and six years later, it still hurts but the pain is not as prominent. I want you to know that the times are ahead are dark and they are cold but they are not times you have to face in isolation. You are never alone.

There's a certain quote from Harry Potter, said by Sirius Black. "The ones that love us never really leave us."

It's heartbreaking and true. As they are remembered they're never truly dead. They live in our memories. And I want you to know that you are loved and that is something worth remembering.

Love, Morgana

CHAPTER 7

N O. 7; A LETTER TO SOMEONE FROM YOUR CHILDHOOD

JANUARY 5th, 2014

Dear Narumi,

Do you miss me? Cause I miss you. I miss us. I miss our childhood more than I need air.

If there is a year of my life, an age I can pinpoint and say, yeah that was the best year of my life, then I would say it was when I was eight.

I had you, you were my best and only friend. I had Evelyn. Our relationship wasn't so messed up then. I didn't hate her, I didn't feel like I was competing with her. Back then, I never felt like she was the sun and I was the insignificant asteroid and most important of all, I had my mother. She was still alive and still the centre of my universe.

Narumi, you were the first friend I ever made.

Do you remember? I was six years old. A little on the chubby side with big eyes and messy pigtails. I was fresh from South Africa and practically shaking with nerves. The two of us were standing in front of the class. Mrs. Yeadon, a woman so thin I worry that she would disappear at any moment, had taken both our hands and led us into the brightly coloured classroom.

"Class," she said in a nasally voice we would often mock, "We have two new students today!"

There was a mixture of blank stares, friendly smiles, a random clap and a few hellos scattered among the class of twenty-four.

She pointed to me, short and chubby me, and said, "This is Morgana! Can you guess where she's from?"

Gregory Bartleby, who now works full time in McDonald's, shouted, "Mars! She looks like an alien!"

Giggles erupted and I ducked my head in embarrassment, burying my face in the woolly scarf that wrapped my neck. Mrs. Yeadon at least had the decency to issue Greg with a stern warning and a lunchtime detention.

"South Africa," she said, "Morgana came all from South Africa," she paused and glanced down at me, smiling kindly, "Where exactly in South Africa was it again love?"

"Pretoria," I told her.

"What?"

"Pretoria," I repeated. I'm laughing right now. God, do you remember how strong my accent was? For the first six months, nobody could understand a word I was saying and for the first six months, I missed Pretoria more than anything. I used to cry almost every day, complaining to my mum about how I wanted to go back to the familiarity of South Africa. To the bruising sunshine and the long summers. England was a labyrinth, a strange new land made of impulsive skies and alien faces. I felt so lost, and I guess what I'm trying to say is that I would never have found my way out of that labyrinth, if you hadn't been by my side. Eleven years later and my accent has dissipated and in its place is a clean cut English accent.

I had to repeat Pretoria about ten times before she understood what I was saying.

She'd smiled again and said, "Welcome to Nottingham, Morgana, I'm hope you'll like it just as much as Pretoria."

Mrs Yeadon did happen to be right about that. After eleven years in Nottingham, I have come to love this city dearly. As frustrating and just downright weird as Nottingham can be, it's my home. And there's no place like home right?

Soon after she turned to you and said, "Well, this is Narumi! She's came yesterday, so she's new as well!"

You were so small and skinny with straight black hair and a shy smile. You weren't from around here either. You had just moved from Japan, from a small city called Miyoshi. Mrs. Yeadon claimed you couldn't speak English properly but I found out three days later that your English was perfect and the reason you lied was because you didn't want to talk to her. I nearly peed myself every time Mrs. Yeadon tried to have a conversation with you. You would always look at her blankly, spouting phrases in Japanese and the occasional broken sentences in English. For almost two years we timed how long it would take until she gave up. It was almost always a minute and forty-two seconds.

As I write this, something heavy is forming in my chest. It's dull and warm and it constricts my heart. I want to go back to those days Narumi. You know, when everything was so much easier?

When the world didn't look so dark and nothing hurt. At eight, my biggest worry was what I would eat for lunch. I couldn't wait to grow up. I couldn't wait to have my own house and a handsome husband and lots of money. At eight, I spent too much time worrying about what others thought of me (I still do) and not enough time with my mother. If I knew this would be my future, I would hug mum a little tighter, I would smile a whole lot brighter and I would have told Michael Yeboah I had a crush on him.

We used to have sleepovers almost every week, I remember we would stay up until the late night, whispering secrets to each other in the dark and giggling at the most juvenile confessions. You and I were inseparable. Well, we were inseparable and then Burbank School happened. Secondary school changed everything.

Life wasn't a walk in the park anymore, life became a jumble of grades, pointless crushes and erratic hormones. Life, for the first time, wasn't yes or no. It was everything in between, nothing was simple and everything hurt. We grew apart in secondary school, you drifted into the cooler cliques, you became one of the celebrities. I became...I don't know what I became but it definitely was not cool. I think was (am) in the middle of popularity and anonymity.

Being Evelyn's sister meant that I was always on the school's radar.

Being Evelyn's sister meant that I always in her shadow.

Within the first three months of Year Seven, you started avoiding me. I would save a seat for you in lessons and you would walk right past me as if I was a ghost and sit next to someone else. That someone else was usually part of the cool crowd. By the beginning of our second year, I finally got the message. I wasn't Sera Hasan, who was undoubtedly the most beautiful girl in our year, and you didn't have time for me. You had outgrown me. Gone on to better things, better people.

Do you remember in Year Nine, when I accidentally bumped into you and you gave me the dirtiest look and called me a freak? I do. Do you remember last year, when I found you crying in the girls' bathroom? I gave you some tissue and stayed with you until you had composed yourself. Do you remember, five months later when the roles reversed and you found me crying in the girls' bathroom and instead of asking me how I was, you momentarily glanced my way and left without a word. I fucking do.

I hope it was worth it. I hope selling your heart and soul, selling all your beliefs and everything that made you so you was worth it. Judging from the rumours spreading about your apparent pregnancy and fallout with Christine Wellington, I don't think it was.

I don't miss you.

I miss the Narumi from primary school. The Narumi that didn't care about the latest trends and the hottest boys. The Narumi who wanted to see the world. There's a part of me that hates you for abandoning me like that, there a part of me that wants to drag you by your expensive extensions and show you all the times I cried and cried about the fact you left me so easily.

What's that song? That song by Gotye.

And now you're just somebody that I used to know.

And now you're just somebody that I no longer wish to know.

Love, Morgana

Chapter 8

No. 8; A LETTER TO YOUR BEST INTERNET FRIEND

JANUARY 13th, 2014

Dear Raven,

Evelyn (and Dad and Jasmin and Ariel) says I spend too much time on my laptop. She says, I need to get off the interweb (she actually said interweb) and go outside and socialise. I always tell her I've already been "outside" and I've "socialised" and it hasn't been much fun.

Yesterday, she barged into my room without even so much as a knock. If I had done that, she would have me hung, drawn and quartered. Of course I wouldn't dare because just last month, I walked into her and Zachariah Baird (who I'm pretty sure is dating Imogen Collins) in the middle of a pretty heated snog session. Raven, they were practically naked and rolling around on her bed. I think I screamed and Evelyn screamed and Zach screamed. I ran out of the room. I had the urge to wash my hands out with soap and bleach and eradicate the picture from my mind. Now I always knock beforehand because I'm afraid of what I might see.

Sorry, I'm rambling.

So, yesterday Evelyn barged straight into my room and started rooting through my wardrobe like she was looking for Narnia. She was throwing my clothes everywhere, not caring about the mess she was making.

"Where are my jeans?" she asked and swivelled to face me. Her hands were on her hips, her perfectly made up eyebrow quirked high. She noticed my confused expression and sighed, "the faded blue skinny jeans I bought like three days ago."

I imitated her exasperated sigh and returned to my laptop, "I don't know."

And I didn't really care because I had this conversation with her so many times. It's always to do with clothes or make-up and how she's lost something or another and how I must have stolen it. I wasn't really listening as she started ranting at me and talking about how important those jeans were if she was going to succeed in outshining Christine Wellington. I didn't care.

You see, my attention was on Tumblr. Raven, you and I both understand how addictive that site is. All I do is reblog things and talk to you. It's funny because I don't have many friends in my real life, and yet when I log onto Tumblr, I have more than I can count. When I'm online talking to you, Aishwarya and Makoto and so many others, I don't feel so...so alone. I feel like I'm part of something, like my voice can be heard. In school and at home, I always end up feeling like this insignificant dot, like nothing I do makes a difference. Do you know what I mean?

You know how when you drop a stone into a pond and it creates a ripple, watery rings spreading and weakening as they rise and fall on the liquid surface. Well, I feel like a stone that is dropped into a pond but makes no ripple, no noise. I simply drop and sink. Sometimes, when my days are darker than usual and everything feels grey, I feel like that stone.

Some days I can feel myself falling, collapsing into the water without even so much as a splash or sound. I try to kick, to swim to do anything but the more I try, the stronger the pull and quicker I sink. My scream swallowed by the salty water that fills my lungs. I sink deeper and deeper into the dark and all I can see, all I can feel are icy fingers yanking me down.

I hate those days.

I could never tell anyone this you see. I can't tell my friends, not Emma or Kali or even Georgia in fear they would judge me. I can't talk to Dad or Jasmin, they wouldn't understand. They would just think it was one of those teenage hormones things and you and I both know there is no chance in hell I would ever talk to Evelyn about this. I doubt she would care and she'd probably call me a freak and tell all her friends about how pathetic I am. Even you Raven, I could talk to you about this but I would only tell you the diluted version, nothing to deep or dark because I couldn't stand anybody knowing something so broken about me.

Oh God, I'm being depressive again. I won't bore you with sob stories Raven. What I'm saying is that, when I go online and I'm blogging on Tumblr, I...I guess I don't feel so insignificant. I don't feel like a stone that doesn't make a ripple you know?

Raven, I wish you didn't live in New Zealand. I wish you were my sister instead of Evelyn. Oh I wish you could see how handsome James looks with his new haircut. It's not as messy anymore and I think he's actually started brushing it (something tells me it's because of Natalie Huxham). You knew about my crush before I even knew myself. You've been telling me for ages to just 'get some balls' and ask him out already and I've been telling you for ages there is no chance in heaven, earth or hell that would ever happen. James and I, we're impossible. I'm scared we might be the only impossible thing in this universe.

Cause, Cher Lewinsky says he's gonna ask Natalie Huxham out soon. They've been hanging out a lot lately and every time I see them, she's always touching his arm or laughs at something he said. He usually smiles back or leans into her. It makes my blood boil and my heart break all at the same time.

Raven, do me a favour, don't give your heart to anyone. Keep it in a cage and that drop that cage into a deep dark chasm where no one will ever find it. You're safer that way.

Y'know, I told you once, I can't stand myself.

Why? you said.

I'm not good enough. I want to be better. How can I be better?

Don't, you said, you already are.

I don't know why I laughed. It sounded like a good joke.

Love, Morgana.

CHAPTER 9

N O. 9; A LETTER TO SOMEONE YOU WISH YOU COULD TALK TO

JANUARY 25th, 2014

Dear Jaz,

You've been married to my dad for four years now. I have to admit, I hated you when we first met. For months, I thought you were trying to take Mum's place, I had convinced myself that you were only interested in Dad for some weird selfish and totally superficial reason. Then, I saw how happy he was around you, how you lifted the darkness that had engulfed him since Mum's death and I realised that you were good for him.

She makes him happy, Ariel once told me, isn't that enough?

She was right. Ariel is always right. For a nine-year-old girl who's obsessed with anything and everything pink, she's freakishly wise.

I've seen the way you and Ariel talk, I've seen how she tells you her worries and you always manage to make her feel like everything will be okay. I wish I could talk to you. I mean, you are qualified therapist and Ariel says you give the best advice. It's just,

I can't bring myself to do it. I'm a very private person.I keep my personal issues to myself, especially those that cut the deepest. I'm too scared to let anyone know about my deepest fears and I couldn't stand anyone knowing those secrets I have kept crumpled and stuffed in the darkest corners of mind.

It's like handing that person a loaded gun and hoping they won't shoot you. Knowledge is power and if I shared my secrets and fears, I feel like they would have power over me, somehow, that they could bring it up at any moment and manipulate me or make me feel ashamed. Jaz, I wish I could talk to you, I wish you could hug me and tell me everything will be okay.

I can't talk to you, so I'm going to write to you.

Jaz, I'm writing this letter in my bedroom. The door is shut, the curtains are closed and Ed Sheeran playing. I had the worst week Jaz. I came from home school about ten minutes ago and grabbed the nearest piece of scrap paper I could find. I just need to get this off my chest, I need to tell someone, anyone before I exploded. God, my handwriting is such a mess and I think I'm about to cry.

Jaz.

Everything feels bland. Everything tastes grey.

For the past couple of weeks I've been feeling like I'm not really here. As if I'm just there. Not mentally or emotionally but physically. I'm on autopilot. I just get through the days. I'm always thinking to myself, just get through today, get through tomorrow, get through this week, get through this damn month if you can.

I used to think I was waiting for something, something big to happen you know? Something that would solidify my life, make everything seem real. But that's not it. It's more like I'm missing something.

There's this, this hollow cave right were my heart should be and it's driving me mad because I don't know how to get rid of it. It's there constantly, even when I'm laughing I can feel it in the recesses of my mind, lurking in the dark, just hidden from plain sight. Some days I can ignore it, I can plaster on a smile and I'll fool myself into thinking it has gone, that everything is fine. But it's not and Jaz, I just...I don't know what to do.

I don't know what's making me feel this void. Why does everything feel so bland and dull and lifeless and why am I losing that ability to care? My energy is dissipating and I don't care. I don't care. I don't care. I don't bloody care.

I cried last night, I don't know. It was past midnight, everybody else had fallen asleep and I just lay in bed, wrapped in darkness and with these thoughts running through my head. They were sharp and vicious and they choked. I felt so helpless and the next thing I knew these deep sobs wracked my body and I started crying. I wept silently. I cried for my mother – I wanted her back, I cried because nothing felt right, because I didn't know what to do with anything, because I hated everything. I wanted to curl up in a ball, I wanted to forget it all. I wanted the night to take me and never return.

I'm just so tired. I need a break. Mostly from myself, from being me. I can't stand it. I can't stand myself. Jaz, I need a break. I need a break so badly. Just five minutes away from reality so I can gather my thoughts.

Did I tell you? Yesterday, I was sitting in the living room and I was watching some YouTube videos on my laptop. More specifically I was watching a clip from Kevin Hart's tour (he's really funny okay?) and Ariel pranced into the room, wearing that fairy costume she loves so much. I laughed at whatever Kevin Hart had just said and I snorted. Ariel looked at me and scrunched up her little nose. She said, "You're really awkward you know that? That's probably why you don't have any friends, you make them feel awkward."

She waved her wand at me, as if she was casting some sort of spell and pranced out of the room. I was feeling so high and then that made me crash down. My smile dropped and those destructively dark thoughts came back in an overwhelming whirlwind. I just sat there and let the thoughts consume me, I let them eat and feed and gorge.

I gave myself two minutes to let the tears fall down my cheeks before I quickly scrubbed them away. She was right. I know, it's pathetic to get upset over something so trivial and especially something said by a nine-year-old but it's true. I am awkward. I am weird. I am pathetic. I don't have any real friends, I don't have anyone to share my deepest fears and darkest secrets, my worries, my hopes and dreams and that ties a chain to my heart and pulls it down into a dark abyss.

Ten minutes after Ariel left the room, you entered and I think you knew I'd been crying. You didn't say anything though, you glanced at me and gave me a concerned look. You knew I would only shut you out and insist everything was fine. So, that's what I did, I forced a smile that felt like cardboard and pretended to be fine.

If I pretend long enough I might start to believe it.

Love, Morgana.

Chapter 10

NO. 10; A LETTER TO SOMEONE YOU WISH YOU COULD MEET

FEBRUARY 2nd, 2014

Dear God,

I'm not religious but I thought you would be a cool guy to talk to. Well, everyone says you are. So, in English Lit we're studying Macbeth (we were supposed to be studying Dr. Faustus but Ms. Kiplin decided that the book was too "challenging" for us as it featured complicated themes, deep philosophical analysis and heavy religious tones some students in the class would not be able to "grasp". But I think she was talking about Christine Wellington because her common knowledge is seriously lacking. I mean, the other day she asked Ms. Kiplin if Jesus was alive in the fifteenth century. I thought this was a stupid decision and I stayed behind after class to try and change her mind but she was set on Macbeth. I mean I don't have a problem with Macbeth, it's an amazing play but I prefer Dr. Faustus because this guy makes a deal with the devil for knowledge and power and Macbeth just deals with some witches. Sorry, I'm going off topic. I tend to do that) and earlier today, I walked into class and sat down in my usual place along Chandra Jayaraman.

On the board I saw Ms. Kiplin had written, If you could meet anyone in history or fiction, who would it be? It was one of those icebreaker activities she did at the beginning of each lesson that I normally found either annoying or a waste of time but today, the question caught my attention. Ms. Kiplin quietened the class and asked the question out loud. Quite a few people put their hands up.

Beatrice Hunt said she would love to meet Sigmund Freud, she wanted to talk to him about his theories like the Oedipus Complex and the Electra Complex and how he even came up with them. Oscar Alvarado said he would want to meet Atticus Finch, a character from To Kill A Mockingbird because he had a priceless wisdom about life and death he would love for him to share. Naveed Krishnamurthy said he would meet Nikolas Telsa because the man was an absolute genius and a total mad scientist. I wasn't surprised when Marlow Powers said she would love to meet John Lennon because everyone knows Marlow is obsessed with him.

Then the question came to James Will. I don't think James was even listening because he'd been engrossed in whatever he was doodling on his notebook ever since lesson started and he seemed pretty confused when Mrs. Kiplin called out his name. I watched as his green-eyed gaze flickered to the question on the board, then for a heart stopping moment to me and then over to Ms. Kiplin.

He was quiet for a second or two before he shrugged. "No one," he said, "the dead are dead and the fictional aren't real, so...I'd rather concern myself with the living. I'd like to meet Alex Turner from the Arctic Monkeys, he's like my favourite guy right now."

I think I must have been smiling or I must have laughed (I don't even know, so many of my actions are involuntarily and rather embarrassing when it comes to James Will) because James glanced at me and smiled back. Did I ever tell you James is my favourite guy ever? Ms. Kiplin frowned at James, obviously not liking his answer and then as I'd dread all lesson, she'd asked me the question. I was still fluttery from the smile he gave me, so I said the first thing that came to mind.

"God," I said.

The silence was suddenly louder than I remembered and I could feel James' gaze on me, a heavy pressure that made my stomach swoop. I hoped I didn't sound like a religious nut.

Ms. Kiplin looked pleasantly surprised. "God? Do you believe in him?"

"No," I said, "but I would like to."

I didn't say anything else. I couldn't bring myself to elaborate why I chose to meet you of all people. People? Is that the right word? Saying people would mean you're human and I don't think that you're human. I think you're on another level. I think you're bigger than this universe, you touch this reality and an infinite amount of others. I was asking myself that question again as I took the bus home. Do I believe in you? I don't. I did once, but I stopped a little while after Mum died. I don't believe you exist anymore. I would really like to because, well, because it must be nice to believe in something.

And I think that if I believed in you, I wouldn't feel so detached. The thing about belief is that it tethers you to something. You can wander but you won't be lost. I think that's the beauty of belief. It gives you a sense of purpose, a direction that shapes everything you do and say.

These days, I'm not so sure what I believe in. I look at the world, a world you supposedly created, and all I see is chaos. And chaos doesn't reward the good and it doesn't punish the bad either. Chaos is chaos and it hides so many things. You see, when I look up at the stars, at the dots of light piercing the darkness through time and space to decorate the black sky, I don't feel awestruck or mesmerised. I feel too small to be significant, and I freeze when I try to think about the sheer and unimaginable size of the universe.

I keep thinking, if you are real, you must be terrifying.

And I keep thinking that if I ever met you, I don't know what I would say to you. Everyone seems to have their conversation with you planned out but honestly, I don't know what I would say to someone with enough power to create something as grand as the universe. But I do think I would start off with why.

Love, Morgana.

CHAPTER 11

N0.11; A LETTER TO A DECEASED PERSON YOU WISH YOU COULD TALK TO

FEBRUARY 7th, 2014

Dear Mum,

Oh God. My hands are shaking as I write this. I don't think you understand how nervous I am right now. Yours is the letter I've been dreading the most because I have so much to say to you that I don't know where to begin and every time I even try to start a letter, I've barely written a sentence before the anxiety and fear and all the grief that's taken so long to wade through comes crashing back in tsunami like waves. Even as this pen scrawls across these pages, I can feel the sorrow rising in my chest and I know it will swallow all the air in my lungs and leave me breathless. Mum. I don't know what to say. I never know what to say. I'm useless like that. I guess —

Shit. I'm crying now.

Shit. Shit. Shit. I thought I could do this. I thought I could write this letter without blubbering like an idiot. I thought I'd put this behind me. I thought I'd shed all the gloom but I think I kept it inside me. I think I've kept all this rage and darkness for so long it's seeped deep into my skin and bones that it's become a part of me. Mum. I guess, there's only three words I can say.

I miss you.

Some days I miss you so much I'm afraid I'll die from the pain. Some days I wish I would.

Mum, please –

No. No. I can't do this.

I can't. I can't stop crying and my tears are soaking the letter, it's messing up the ink.

I'm sorry. I'm so sorry.

I thought I could do this but I can't. I'm weak. I thought I was iron but really I'm glass.

I'm sorry. I'll try again. I promise.

Love, Morgana.

CHAPTER 12

N O.12; A LETTER TO THE PERSON YOU HATE THE MOST

FEBRUARY 8th, 2014

Dear Me,

Is it sad that it didn't take me long to decide who it was I hated the most? Is it sad that person happens to be me? I mean, that has to be just a little tragic right? But, c'mon, who else was it going to be? And what is humanity when it's not tragic?

You know, for a second, I thought it might be Evelyn or Christine or even Narumi but it's not. Sure, I don't like them but it's not this consistent throbbing flow of hatred. It's closer to distaste, the kind that makes your mouth tighten into a grimace. No, I don't hate them. I don't think I really and truly hate anyone. Well, anyone who isn't me. I didn't truly realise that until yesterday.

It was after I'd failed to write that letter to Mum. I'd scrunched the paper up with tears streaking my face and thrown it across the room. A harsh, burning wave of shame crashed over me and I fell back onto my bed. I dug the heels of my hands into my eyes but it didn't stop the tears from spilling. I'd never felt so disgusted with myself. I'd never felt so weak and worthless as I did in that wretched moment. I kept asking myself what was wrong with me. Why couldn't I write one letter to my mother? Just one fucking letter. That was all. Just one letter. One letter. Just let her know I loved her. Tell her everything I'd meaning to say since she died, everything I never got the chance to say before she died and everything I couldn't say after she died.

I wanted to scream, I wanted to wail like a banshee because it was all building up in my chest but I couldn't. Not when Evelyn was next door with Nadia Tawfeek and Rosanna Keitel. They're the biggest gossips in sixth form and God knows, Evelyn would feel mortified if they knew her sister was having a breakdown. I couldn't let them hear me crying. It would be like walking straight into a den packed with hyenas. They would see me in this state and they would devour me. So, I bit my tongue and held it in. The fear of being seen so shattered kept the scream at bay. All I could do was cry silently into my hands and as I lay there, my breathing ragged and my chest heavy with a raging sort of darkness, the face of the enemy emerged from the chaos.

It wasn't Jasmin. It wasn't Evelyn. It wasn't my father. It wasn't Kyle Witter or Sera Hasan.

It was me.

My own pallid face stared back at me in the darkness and I finally knew my enemy. What are you supposed to do when you find out something like that? Do you celebrate? Is there anything worth celebrating when you find out the great darkness in your life is not some force created by the universe or some sneering man in the periphery of your vision, but that it's you. You are the great darkness. I am my own despair. What do you do when you find out you are your own demons. I am the nightmare I have been fearing all these years.

What do you do? What am I supposed to do with that kind of information? Someone tell me. I don't know what to do. I don't know what to do. Oh God. What's the use in asking myself? I'm useless. I feel so lost and unknown. I feel like I'm drowning and I don't have the will to save myself. I think I might just let myself sink and sink until I'm buried so deep in the chasm and the darkness is so dense, the memory of light is just that, a memory.

I'll tell you what I did when I realised the enemy I'd been struggling to find for so long was me. I cried. I dug the heels of my hand harder into my eyes and I cried silent, feverish sobs. I wanted to claw my eyes out and scream and weep and disappear into nothingness. I don't know how long I stayed like that but I must have fallen asleep at some point. I startled awake to resounding silence and the bleak black sky peaking at me through my curtains. My phone told me it was half one in in the morning. Everyone in the house had already gone to bed.

I had a splitting headache from all the crying, so I rummaged through the drawers and downed a couple tablets of Nurofen. The heaviness in my chest was still there and I doubted it would leave any time soon. I pushed the curtains open a little wider so I could look out onto the empty street. I briefly wondered if I was the only one awake. A few houses down to my right, the living room light was still on and I saw a silhouette moving about. My eyes soon wandered up to the night sky. The stars blinked down at me and I wondered what they thought of humanity. What they thought of me. I wondered if there were gods nestled in the stars and if they had been watching us all these centuries. They must be bored by now. Watching us make the same mistakes over and over again.

I turned around and grabbing a notebook and pen from my bag, I sat back down on my bed and I started to write this letter. So, here I am. It's nearly two o'clock in the morning and I'm writing this letter in the dim light of the moon.

I'm not going to sit here and list out all the things I hate about myself because what would be the point? I don't think I can cry anymore. My body feels too barren to grow sadness. Maybe – maybe, I should try and figure out why I feel that way or maybe I should go to a therapist. But the idea of someone poking around in my head like that is unsettling. I guess I'll just have to figure this whole thing out on my own. I have to defeat my demons. So, now, I guess the million dollar question is...

How do you do defeat yourself?

Love, Morgana.

CHAPTER 13

N0.13; A LETTER TO THE PERSON THAT PESTERS YOUR MIND, GOOD OR BAD

FEBRUARY 10th, 2014

Dear James,

We've known each other for almost two years now and in that time you've come to be a good friend. You might not know this but you're very dear to me, James, so close to my heart that the drumming beat must have deafened you long ago. Despite all this, I do think you're a pest. I'm always thinking about you.

Last night, as I shoved my clothes into the washing machine, I heard Breakfast at Tiffany's by Deep Blue Something playing in the living room and I had sudden flash of you. Sitting in the common room with earphones in as you mumbled along to the song. I watched you for a while, your fingers tapping your knee and your head bobbing ever so slightly. It was such an endearing image, it had the corners of my mouth pulling up into a wide grin. You're the most endearing thing, James.

I thought of you again today in third period Politics (a subject you should be thankful you didn't take). Mr Medeiros was showing the class a PowerPoint on utopian socialism but I wasn't paying attention. I was staring out of the window, at the spring blue sky that made me think of a picture of you. You'd posted it on your Facebook last year, when you went to Greece in the summer holidays. You had been surrounded by clear blue skies and sun, sand and sea. You were lounging on a deck chair with your hands clasped behind your back and that lazy grin on gracing your handsome features. Your eyes were hidden behind a pair of sunglasses but I could tell they were half squinting in that way when you're close to laughing. It was the first time I'd seen you topless and I'd noted with a slightly parted mouth that you had a very nice body. Broad shoulders and tanned, sun-kissed skin. You were gorgeous.

I think of you when I walk past a field of tulips or see a bird fluttering in the trees or hear the sound of rain outside my window because you once told me spring was your favourite season. Everything is new and beautiful and coming to life after harsh seasons. I think of you when I'm laughing because I hope you're watching and falling in love with my laugh too. I think of you when I lie in bed and wonder what it would be like to fall asleep in your arms. I think of you when I'm walking to school and wishing you were by my side. I think of you when I'm biting into a slice of mango and I wonder if your lips would taste just as sweet.

I keep thinking of you and it's maddening, James.

It's maddening to have you in my head all the time, you're a broken record that keeps replaying. It's a song I've heard a thousand times before and it's a song I won't mind hearing another thousand.

Love, Morgana.

CHAPTER 14

N0.14; A LETTER TO SOMEONE YOU DRIFTED AWAY FROM

FEBRUARY 14th, 2014

Dear Evelyn,

William Somerset Maugham said, "The great tragedy of life is not that men perish, but that they cease to love." It got me thinking about you. About us. About how close we used to be when we were younger. It made me wonder if that was us now. If we had forgotten any reason to love each other and replaced them with reasons why we should hate one other instead.

It's gotten to the point where we can't be in the same room without getting into some kind of argument and I'm worried our poison will spill onto Ariel. She's not stupid, she's beginning to notice the way we treat each other, like we're strangers unfortunately tied together by blood. A bond we would do anything to sever. We may not have the best relationship but I think we do try to show Ariel we love her.

I've seen you brushing her hair or teaching her how to cook some of your favourite dishes. You helped her make her fairy costume for her school play, I mean, you were the whole reason she even got that part. You gave her the confidence to get on stage and sing. You were the first person to rise up out of your seat and clap for her. There was so much pride in your smile that day and Ariel stood on stage with the poise of someone who'd just conquered the world. Ariel adores you and I can tell by the way your eyes light up when she shows you a new dance she learnt that you love her too.

I like to watch movies with her (particularly movies from the early 2000s like Mean Girls, About A Boy, and The Princess Diaries) and I introduced her to the world of literature, to books that made me feel wild and free. You can learn so much about the world and yourself with books. As Lisa Kleypas once wrote, "A well-read woman is a dangerous creature." My greatest achievement so far is that I finally got her to start reading the Harry Potter series. When she finished The Chamber of Secrets yesterday, she barged into my room and asked me with an excited squeal where the third book was.

I told her I would give her the third book if she'd let you tuck her into bed for the next week. You used to do that all the time when she was a baby but ever since she turned ten a few weeks ago, Ariel's been wanting to tuck herself in. You'd chuckled and rolled your eyes but I could see the disappointment in the set of your shoulders and the faint grimace on your lips.

I heard from Nadia Tawfeek that you and Sean Neumann broke up. The reasons are unknown but rumour has it (by rumour I mean Nadia Tawfeek) he ended it because you were frigid. For two weeks you were cold and harsh and you locked yourself in your room. When you're hurt, Evelyn, you make sure everyone else is hurting too. You're the type of person who would set the world of fire if it meant you weren't the only one burning. I thought if you ever broke it would be the most satisfying thing I'd ever seen but if anything, it was tragic.

I remember finding you in the kitchen, you were staring at your mobile with a forlorn look.

"Are you okay?" I asked, and when your dark eyes flashed to mine, cold and unforgiving, I knew I shouldn't have said anything.

Your lips opened in a snarl, "Why the fuck do you care?"

"I...I heard you and Sean–"

"Mind your own fucking business, Morgana," you snapped.

I took a step back, "Evelyn, I'm just trying to–"

"To what?"

I frowned, "I don't know, I just thought you needed someone to talk to you."

"I don't need anyone, Morgana," you said, and glared at some spot in the distance, "Everyone thinks I'm a bitch just 'cause I don't take their any of their shit and that Sean's angel, so he deserves better than me."

You laughed but it was bitter and you almost sounded like wounded animal.

"Well let me tell you something, Sean Neumann is a dirty low life. You know why I broke up with him? Because he called you a pathetic little parasite but he said he would still totally shag you if you paid him at least fifty quid," you groaned in disgust, "So I punched him in his fucking face 'cause no one talks about my sister like that! And now...now he's going round telling people that he broke up with me because I'm frigid." You threw your hands up in the air. "Me? Frigid? Is he fucking high? You can ask Zachariah Baird and he'll tell you just how –" you paused to do air quotation marks, "frigid I am! Sean Neumann is a godless son of a bitch and if I ever see him again I'm going to crack his head open with a hammer!"

You were breathing hard by the time you finished your rant and I was staring at you with wide eyes as I processed what you'd just said.

"You...You broke up with Sean Neumann because of me?" I asked, not quite believing what I'd just heard.

You frowned, "You might be annoying but you're still my sister, anyway, I'm the only one who's allowed to take the piss out of you Morgana, not some creepy bastard like Sean Neumann."

I was practically gawping at you now, "I...I...uh...Thanks?"

"Yeah, whatever," You said with a roll of your eyes and walked out of the kitchen.

After I'd gotten over the initial shock of you actually defending me, I told Ariel to ask you to tuck her into bed a few days later. I knew if you tucked Ariel into bed it would thaw out the frost in you. And it did, after a few nights of tucking Ariel in, you had forgotten all about Sean and you were back to your old brazen self. I was actually glad to see the return of your trademark smirk and the enchanting way you held everyone's attention.

Earlier today, I found the old family album and started looking through it. I don't know why I never noticed this, but we're together in almost every picture. There's one where we're standing outside our old house in Pretoria. The photograph is dated June 17th, 2001. So, I'm four and you're six years old and Ariel won't be born for another three years. I'm guessing we'd just come from church because Mum's dressed us in matching flowery dresses and shiny white shoes. I'm looking up at the camera with a smile and you have your arms wrapped around me as you give the camera the same elated smile. I thought Narumi was the first friend I ever made but that's not true.

Looking back, I realise the first friend I ever had was you. Evelyn, do you remember a time when all we shared wasn't a rushing flow of bad blood and cutting remarks? I have a vague, almost battered recollection of a time like that. It feels like it was a million worlds away. The photograph captured a moment of blistering happiness, when we weren't enemies but sisters. I really loved you then. I loved you more than anything but then something broke and now I can't remember the last time I didn't feel resentment towards you.

I've been trying to pinpoint exactly when our relationship fell apart and I think it was sometime after Mum died. The cracks started showing when she was sick and everything collapsed the night of her funeral. We screamed at each other, blaming the other for her death until we could no longer form words. I wish there was a way to get back to the way we were. Over the years we've been drifting further and further from each other, we've wandered so far I can barely see you anymore. We're oceans apart and I'm afraid that one day you'll become a memory, a ghost and I don't want that. Evelyn, I would cross all the oceans in the world to get back to you.

Something tells me I might be able to because this morning, when I dredged up the courage to say good morning you didn't throw me your cold stare or ignore me like you usually did.

You looked at me and said, "Oh hey, Morgana."

For the first time in so long, we ate breakfast without bickering, we ate in an easy silence. But the thing that took me most by surprise is when you finished your toast, you paused in doorway and said, "Hey, do you want a lift to school?"

I blinked in surprise because normally, I would have to walk twenty-five minutes with only my iPod for company. I nodded, "Er...yeah...I would, thanks."

"Cool, I'm going in ten minutes so be ready."

You left me alone in the kitchen with a disbelieving smile on my face as I went back to eating my cereal.

Evelyn, I don't think we can get back to the way we were but I think we can move forward. Maybe it's not too late to rebuild the bridge we burnt down. And maybe, crossing the oceans that keep us apart won't be so hard if you meet me halfway.

Love, Morgana.

CHAPTER 15

N 0.15; A LETTER TO SOMEONE THAT'S NOT IN YOUR COUN-
TRY

FEBRUARY 19th, 2014

Dear DC,

It's a shame you had to move half way across the world. It's a shame I didn't say goodbye, so this letter will have to do. You left the same summer we finished Year Eleven. You told me on the day of our GCSE French exam that you and your family were leaving to go live in Australia. You have to admit that was bad timing. You could have at least told me after.

We were waiting outside the exam hall, a class of twenty-five pupils bubbling with nerves. For most of us there, it would be our first exam. I sat at the bottom of the staircase that led to the science block. I'd wanted to get some last minute revision in so I'd brought my French textbook and placed it on my lap. It was easy to block out all the chatter, everyone kept asking each other if they'd revised or not and they kept saying just how glad they would be once these exams were over so they could sleep for fifteen hours a day and go out with their mates. I didn't want to socialise since I'd made myself a resolution to at least get a B in French.

Somehow, don't ask me how, your voice, clear and crisp cut through the world I'd encased myself in. I glanced up and you were standing before me with your hands stuffed in your pockets and an eyebrow raised pointedly at me.

"Morgs," you tutted and shook your head, "Cramming before an exam is weak. You either know your shit or you don't."

Morgs. I never liked that nickname. It was something you named an ogre. Of course you knew this and kept at it but now you're gone I find myself missing it. I miss the way it would roll of your tongue and I miss the quick smirk you would give me when I told you to call me Morgana.

"We'll see who the weak one is on results day, DC," I said.

Everybody called you by your surname because you were the third Francis in our year. You wouldn't have cared so much if I hadn't started calling you Dawson's Creek in Year Eight. It annoyed you so much and you always got this adorable, almost confused little crease between your eyebrows so I kept doing it. You didn't think it was funny but I thought it was hilarious. Especially when everybody else started adopting my little nickname and before you know it, your name had been shortened to DC by the beginning of Year Nine. You said you much preferred DC since it not only made you sound like a rapper but that you were happy to rep DC Comics since they were a godsend.

You shrugged, "Might not be here on results day. I might have them mailed to me."

"Why?" I said, only half-listening as I flickered through the text-book, "Are you on holiday?"

"Nah, I'm...I'm moving away actually."

I froze and slowly looked up at you. You carded a hand through your black hair and offered me a slanted grin.

"What?" I said.

"My aunt's got a job offer at some Australian television network as a head writer for a new show," you said, "it's a great opportunity and it's been her dream for so long, plus...the pay isn't too bad."

I remember you telling me you lived with your aunt and uncle ever since your parents had passed away a few years ago. You never told me how you lost them. I didn't want to push you. You didn't carry your grief like I did. You swallowed your grief whole and drowned the taste with something bitter. I think that's why we became such good friends, DC. We recognised a loss within ourselves and built a sturdy if not haply made bridge to cross the chasm and come together.

You understood the gnawing detachment like nobody else and I think over the years, over our early morning walks to school and our teasing between classes, you became an integral part of my life.

"Wh-Where in Australia?" I said, trying to sound nonchalant when my blood was roaring in my ears.

"Melbourne," you said.

"Well, are you coming back?"

"Nah, staying there," you said, running another hand through your black hair, "it's just sun, sand and Australian babes, who are total suckers for an English gentleman like myself."

I didn't say anything for about ten seconds, my mind felt static as I tried to process what I'd just heard.

"Oh."

I sounded like an arse but it was all I could manage to say.

"Yeah," you replied just as lamely.

We stared at each other for a couple seconds, your dark eyes boring into mine and my own boring into yours. You opened your mouth to say something, my heart fluttered for some reason in anticipation but Mr Weinstein cut you off.

"The exam is about to begin," he said in a droning voice. "Everybody needs to get in an orderly line and come into the exam hall. I want silence upon entry, anybody that disturbs the exam gets to miss out on prom."

Everybody started moving except us, we stayed locked in each other's gaze for a few seconds longer. There was a question in the air. It was so tangible I could almost taste it, like copper on the tip of my tongue. You opened your mouth once more to speak and I thought the hanging question was finally going to be snipped from the wire and dropped but Mr Weinstein cut you off again.

"Dawson! Jones!" his sharp voice made us both jump, "Stop loitering and get in the hall, unless you want to miss your exams?"

You frowned and shot him a glare. I got up and hastily shoved my textbook into my bag and fell into step behind you. Every so often in the exam, I kept glancing at you and you would do the same. We went back to our usual selves and didn't really talk about the fact you were leaving. I think you were happy I didn't pester you with questions or try to drag you to some party to say farewell because on most days, you would find me and just sit down next to me without saying a word. We would stay like that for a while, savouring a silence so many people feared. Sometimes, you would glance at me and give me a soft, easy smile and I would smile back.

There was always an understanding between us, DC, a recognition, a vague sense of home I never had with anyone else.

When Results Day came on that cloudy August day, everybody ripped open their letters. I was happy with my results, more than happy actually I was elated. Three As, Five Bs and two Cs. One of those B's was in French by the way, I'd just scraped it in. I waited for you most of the day to show you my victory dance as I flashed my B but you never turned up.

Georgia must have seen my forlorn expression since she told me what I already knew.

"He left for Australia a few days ago," she'd said and seemed to match my sadness when she sighed, "I really wanted to say goodbye but...yeah."

Georgia had a crush on you back then. She'd liked you since you'd picked that leaf out of her hair in Year Seven and had been working up the courage to ask you out ever since. She would kill me if she found out I told you that. Then again, I'm not really telling you anything. I might as well be speaking to a wall because you are never going to get this letter. But that's not reason I write these letters. They're more for me than anybody else.

I think Cher Lewinsky had a crush on you as well. So did Nadia Tawfeek and Clementine Godford come to think of it, actually I'd say at least half the girls in our year had some sort of crush on you, DC. There were all so depressed when you left. I don't know how you got those girls' hearts to beat for you but I bet it had something to do with that bad boy thing you had going. You know what I'm talking about. The way you smirked and walked in mystery like you had a secret nobody could ever guess. The thing is nobody really knew anything about you except that you were Francis Dawson, you had an affinity for the Black Keys and you got into a lot of trouble. You were the big question everyone was desperate to answer.

Last time I saw you, we were sixteen. Do you remember? It was the second week of June and we'd just finished our last exam, you had R.E and I had History. You'd invited me back to yours to "chill or whatever, I'm bored," so we'd walked home together in the baking heat. You lived in an apartment complex near town, it was nice, very modern and made up of greys and whites. You offered me some of your uncle's beer but I declined and stuck with the can of coke. Your aunt and uncle were at work, so we hung out in the living room listening to music and talking about God knows what for hours.

"Are you scared?" I'd asked you as Lana Del Rey played in the background. "About Australia."

You paused, the beer inches from your lips, and shrugged. "I don't know," you said, "I thought I would be, but...I guess I'm ready to leave this place y'know? I feel...I feel beyond it."

"Oh," I said, somehow disappointed because it wasn't the answer I'd expected.

Your dark brown eyes flitted over to me then. There was curiosity flickering in them and then something deeper, something I couldn't quite pinpoint but it made me feel alive with nerves.

"But not you."

"What?"

"I don't feel beyond you," You said and your mouth parted into a crooked grin, "Don't let this go to head but I might miss you, Morgs."

I returned your grin, "I might miss you too, DC."

When your aunt came home from work, she seemed surprised to see me there. Apparently you didn't really bring people over to the flat, she was so excited she invited me to stay for dinner. It was weird. Not the dinner or your aunt, I mean, seeing you outside of school, outside the uniform. At school your were aloof and bored by everything but at home you were bright and electric and I could suddenly see how you had stolen some many girls' hearts.

After dinner, you walked me home. We didn't live far from one another, it was about fifteen minutes by foot. When we stood outside my door, your dark eyes flicked up at the waning moon and then back to me.

"Word of advice," you said, "Don't be so hard on yourself. I can see it sometimes, the war in you, it's the same one I've been fighting ever since my parents died. I know you probably don't want to hear this but...You'll be okay. My uncle says the best path to redemption is forgiveness." You had a serious, almost resolute look on your face I'd never seen before. You placed a hand on my shoulder and gave it a gentle squeeze. "Morgana, you need to accept your mistakes and know they don't define you."

I swallowed hard as I stared at you, lost for words. "S-Since when did you get so wise?"

Your hand left my shoulder and you chuckled. "Didn't you know? I'm the new Yoda." You shoved your hands in your jacket pockets and your eyes didn't leave mine as you took a couple of steps back. You gave me a mock salute and in the moonlight, I could the sharp smirk on your lips.

"I'll catch you later, Morgs," You said and turned around.

I watched you go as I felt every shade of blue swarm in my chest. I couldn't form the words in my mouth, I physically couldn't bring myself to say goodbye, so I just waved. I guess I thought I would see you again but I didn't. It's been two years since that night and I haven't seen you.

You're going to be eighteen on the ninth of March. Is it sad I remember your birthday after two years? I think everything in my life has an undertone of melancholy.

I'd like to wish you happy birthday but you deleted your Facebook in Year Ten. You dropped me a text on my seventeenth last year. It was close to midnight and sleep was moments away until my phone buzzed me awake. It was an unexpected phenomena that had my heart racing as I stared at my phone in the dark.

Happy birthday Morgs!

I didn't recognise the number but I knew it was you. You were the only one you called me Morgs. I saved the message, I couldn't delete it. So, I'm going to do the same for you, DC. When the calendar reaches the ninth of March, I'll wish you happy birthday and a wonderful life because you deserve the night sky and more, DC.

Shit, this letter is turning out to be longer than I expected. I guess I had a lot more to say to you than I thought.

Sometimes, I'll look up at the moon and I like to think you're looking at it too. It makes me feel less lonely, knowing that you might be on the other end of the world but you still staring up at the same moon. At least the moon will always be ours to share.

I miss you. I do. I really do. You were one of my closest friends (as much you didn't like to admit it) and I miss you dearly. Australia must be a nice change to England. I'd say a lot of people would exchange Nottingham for Melbourne. I know I would if it meant I could see you again.

I think I will.

See you again that is. I realise now that must have been the question hanging in the air that day.

Will I see you again?

That's what you meant to ask me isn't it?

We're connected you and I, by some string that transcends distance and time. I will see you again, it might not be today or tomorrow or even in a decade but we will meet again. And I think when we do, it'll be like coming home.

Love, Morgana.

CHAPTER 16

NO.16; A LETTER TO SOMEONE YOU WISH COULD FORGIVE YOU

FEBRUARY 24th, 2014

Dear Me,

Today, I somehow wound up watching an episode of Jeremy Kyle and after arguing for about a minute with one of the guests (he does that a lot), Jeremy asked him and the audience if they could name one person they wish could forgive them. A person in the audience named his brother, he said he regretted not going to his wedding because of a misplaced sense of pride. The guest, a man in his mid-thirties who had slicked back greasy hair and wore a fake Ralph Lauren polo shirt named a boy from his childhood. Apparently, he'd let the boy get bullied when he could have stopped it and he's been seeking forgiveness ever since.

And it got me thinking. Who do I wish could forgive me? I started rattling off the people in my life, the names and faces I'd known over the years but there was no cutting guilt that told me forgiveness was needed. And then I thought back to a few weeks ago when I was weeping in my room over my failed attempt to write Mum a letter and I realised, maybe – maybe the person I wished could forgive was me.

I'm so tired of this bubbling wave of self-hatred that sits under the surface, waiting and waiting to erupt. I read somewhere that guilt is good. It's good because it encourages empathy and it gives you the urge to make amends. You have to deal with your guilt before it's too late or it will end up devouring you. I'm afraid it might devour me and in a sick kind of way, I almost want it to. I want to be devoured and left so hollow the end of my existence is seconds away. But I can't let that happen. I won't. I have to find this illusive path of self-forgiveness and walk through it and keep walking for how longer it takes, even when my body aches and my feet bleed I have to keep going. I have to keep going forward. I have to wade through my bleak desolation. I have to understand.

The art of self-forgiveness is so foreign it almost seems alien to me. I've forgiven others so many times over the years that it feels like second nature. That's the key word there, others. So, that's the great mystery in my life. How do you forgive yourself? Is that the first step to conquering your demons? Is that how you defeat yourself?

Maybe in order to move forward, I have to go move back. I have to understand my past and how it has brought me here. I have to understand myself and to do that I have to look in not out. If the only way out is in, then I am my own salvation.

Looking into myself is something I've always feared because I'm afraid of what I might find. Discovering yourself seems like an awfully dark adventure. What if it makes me hate myself even more? Do I really want to know who I am or am I content with this half-formed version I have conjured up for others? All these questions and no answer in sight. DC was right, I think the key here is acceptance. I need to accept that I've made mistakes because to err is human. Mistakes are inevitable but I can choose whether or not I learn from them.

I don't want to be my own enemy more. It's tiring and I can't do it anymore. Hate is a poisonous thing and I no longer wish to live in it. I seek forgiveness and for the first time in my life I realise it's not from others but from myself. I want to forgive myself because it might be the key to – to everything. The world would unlock before my eyes and I would stop snarling at myself long enough to see everything in colour. The sky would be bluer, the ice cream sweeter, my laugh brighter and all because the poison within me seeped out and stopped darkening my vision.

Forgiveness is not something that happens overnight, it's a long journey filled with longer days and longer nights but it's a journey I'm willing to make.

Love, Morgana.

CHAPTER 17

N0.17; A LETTER TO YOUR BOYFRIEND, GIRLFRIEND OR SIGNIFICANT OTHER

MARCH 8th, 2014

Dear James,

Yes, I know you're not my boyfriend but a girl can dream right? To tell you the truth, I've never even had a boyfriend let alone a first kiss. Is that weird? I'm seventeen years old and you would think I would have had some romantic or sexual interaction with a boy.

Well, I haven't.

Actually, the closest I have ever gotten to anything remotely romantic is with you. Like that time in Year Twelve. It was in late May and we had a little more than a month of school left before the summer holidays and our first year of sixth form ended. Do you remember? We were sitting at the back of the school library, revising for our English Lit exam that was only four days away. We'd been meeting up every Wednesday afternoon to study together. It had been your idea, you'd suggested it a month before and I'd nodded casually and when you'd run off to catch the bus, I walked all the way home with the brightest smile on my face.

Do you remember, James? Our table were coated with textbooks and notebooks and scraps of highlighted paper. I was looking over my old essays and taking note of the suggestions Ms. Kiplin had made on how to improve and get higher a grade, when you spoke up.

"I'm going to fail," you said.

I looked over at you, you were sitting opposite me. You had this pained look on your face, it pulled your eyebrows together and pressed your mouth into a fine line. You had Macbeth in your hands, and you stared at it like you were ten seconds away from hacking it to pieces with an axe.

"Why do you think that?" I asked.

You continued staring at the book, "I can't do this. I don't know why I thought I could. Shit, I'm going to fail."

I recognised something in your tone, it sounded like despair, the cutting cold kind. If you let that sit inside you long enough, it bleeds into your bones, and eventually rips into your soul. You're too bright for that, James. I couldn't let that kind of misery consume you. I mean, you don't wanna end like me. I felt clawing panic for a moment as I tried to find the right words to drive away your despair. I almost wanted to crack a joke but I knew it wasn't the time for that.

"You know, there's a passage everyone thinks is by Nelson Mandela but it was actually written by Marianne Williamson, she's a spiritual activist and founder of the Peace Alliance," I said but you still weren't looking at me, your eyes were burning holes into the pages of Macbeth. "In one chapter of her book she says something interesting....she says, uh, she says....Our deepest fear is not that we are inadequate. Our deepest fear is that we are powerful beyond measure. It is our light, not our darkness that most frightens us."

And then you must have recognised something in my tone because you slowly looked up. Your green eyes found mine.

"I'm going to repeat something you've heard so many times that it must be ingrained in your system," I said and swallowed, the intensity of your gaze was a heavy pressure that made my heart drum hard. "Life is hard. You know that. Life is hard but...but that doesn't mean you're not. If life gets harder then so do you with each trial you face. These exams might seem tough, James, but you're tougher."

I said, "You're more capable than you think. Like, do you remember when we had our mock exams and you were convinced you were going to fail but you ended up getting one of the highest marks in sixth form? Failure is a powerful motivation to succeed but failing itself is not always a bad thing. In fact, it's from failure that we learn our most important lessons. So don't fear failure, you need it."

You continued to stare at me as I continued talking. I held your gaze as strongly as you held mine because this was important. James, I needed you to understand.

"Your favourite film is The Pursuit of Happyness right?" I asked even I already knew the answer.

You nodded, not saying a word.

"You told me it was your favourite film of all time because it wasn't just inspirational, for you it eliminated any notion of the impossible. Nothing was out of reach. Everything could be yours. It taught you about perseverance and hope," I sighed and tucked loose strands of hair behind my ear, "I...I know I'm rambling but...I...I guess what I...I guess what I'm trying to say is that...you can do anything you want James and you know that. You're nothing less than brilliant. And life doesn't get harder. You do."

A pregnant pause followed my rambling speech and I tried very, very hard not to stare at your parted lips.

I cleared my throat and gave you a small smile. "Okay?"

You nodded once. Then twice before the corners of your mouth rose slowly into a smile that reminded of sunrises. "Okay," you said, your deep voice was a smooth, calming tone.

I gave you a curt nod. I could still feel your gaze on me even as I went back to reading my old essays. I could still feel your smile too, aimed right at me, like sunrays beaming in through the windows and warming my chilly skin. It was a little distracting.

After, when the clocks reached fifteen minutes past two and it was time for fourth period, we packed up our things and left the library. It was when we were outside the double doors of the common room that you reached forward and grabbed my wrist. Do you remember what you did, James? I think you do but I don't think you realise the impact it had on me. I'd turned around, my gaze skipping from the fingers you'd wrapped around my wrist and up to your face.

"Morgana," you said and my pulse spiked because I'd never heard you say my name like that. Like it was the answer to a question you never knew asked.

"Yeah?" I breathed, surprised I could even make a sound.

You smiled that same sunrise smile. "Thank you."

You leaned forward then – your fingers were strong and warm on my wrist, there was the distance sound of chatter, you smelt like sandalwood and forest rain, my blood was roaring past my ears – and placed a gentle kiss on my cheek – your lips were a soft, pressing heat on my skin, my eyes were wide, your grip on my wrist tightened for a moment. You pulled away in a second or two, a lazy summer's day grin on your face. I think I might imagined it in my shocked state but I could have sworn your fingers trailed down my hand as you let go of my wrist. No. Yeah. I must have imagined it.

"I gotta head to Maths but I'll see you later yeah?" you said with that lazy grin.

The spot you'd kissed on my cheek was burning. I nodded. "Yeah...Yeah, later."

You turned and headed downstairs to your lesson, completely unaware of the fact you'd almost sent me into cardiac arrest with that kiss. I wasn't really able to concentrate the rest of the day because the memory of your lips on my cheek, soft and warm, was too much. You're too much James. I know it was just friendly peck to show your gratitude or whatever but that was probably the most romantic thing that's ever happened to me. It felt like the universe had crumpled in on itself until there was only you.

Sometimes, I like to imagine what it would be like if you were my boyfriend. I like to imagine us walking to class hand in hand. I like to imagine your arms around my waist as we make breakfast together. I like to see us hanging out in your bedroom, curled up in your bed watching old movies and talking until dawn breaks over England. I like to imagine what you look like in the mornings, your brown hair all mussed up and your voice must sound even deeper when its heavy with sleep. I like to imagine us pillow fighting and then kissing you to make you smile because I know you're a sore loser. I like to imagine us slow dancing in the living room to a song on the radio. I like to imagine myself walking around school in your bomber jacket that's one size too big for me. I like to imagine and imagine and then I like to shatter my fantasies with the cold, unforgiving reality.

You are not mine and I am not yours.

I repeat it to myself.

You are not mine and I am not yours.

I repeat it to myself until my heart is close to breaking.

You are not mine and I am not yours.

I thank God you'll never know how I feel about you. There's comforting relief in knowing there's no chance between us, that there is a small likelihood you would feel the same because that would be too good James. And you're too good for this world. The very idea is terrifying. It's – it's impossible. You and I are impossible.

A part of me, the sickly, masochistic side even hopes you don't feel the same way. That part wants me to rot in my own isolation. I don't know what I would do if you did like me as well. I might run for the hills and never come back. I once thought it was because I didn't deserve you but I don't think that's it. The world doesn't work like that does it? Not everyone gets what they deserve. No, it's that I don't want to deserve you. I don't want to feel this way any longer. I want you to give me my heart back because you've had it for too long now.

God. James. I've been bearing this crush for almost two years now and I'm beginning to buck under the weight of it all. Sixth form will come to an end in five months and we'll be off to universities, going down our separate paths. I'm hoping the space will give me a chance to get over you.

Do you want to know the truth? I'm scared. I'm scared I might always feel this way about you. I'm scared it might always be you. There's something about you feels that infinite. James, I think my feelings for you may have matured from a simple little crush to something more profound. It thrums through my veins and it burns brighter, hotter. Sometimes, when I look at you, I feel as if my heart is beating so fast it's going to explode from all crackling electricity bursting through it.

James, I'm afraid I might –

I think I –

I can't bring myself to even say the words but I think you can guess.

Love, Morgana.

CHAPTER 18

N O.18; A LETTER TO A PERSON THAT YOU KNOW IS GOING THROUGH HARD TIMES

MARCH 11th, 2014

Dear Laurel,

For the past couple of weeks, you haven't been yourself. I haven't heard any of your sardonic comments or witty remarks in a while and I never thought I'd say this but I actually miss your comebacks. Even though I would never admit this to your face, you're probably the wittiest person I have ever met. No one really stands a chance when it comes to debates. You have a way of turning things on their head and making people see what they've been missing. You have this peculiar ability to both enlighten and oppress. To be honest you were the main reason I joined the debating team. It was in the early November of Year Nine when you took part in the Regional Finals with three other people from our school against some grammar school from Manchester.

I wanted to see what you were like outside our usual banter, if you were as good as everyone said you were and honestly, Laurel, you blew me away. You'd cut through the other team's arguments like a blade and you left me in awe. You showed me the power of words and I remember thinking, sticks and stones may break your bones but words will break your soul. You have this way of crafting words into arrows, into swords, into bullets, into explosives and I thought if knowledge was power, then you had to be the most powerful person in that room.

No one in school really bothered to get into arguments with you, not when you could easily annihilate them within thirty seconds. Well, Zoe Cooper tried in the middle of Year Eleven and she ended up bursting into tears and we didn't see her for three days. I bet Georgia and Adeola ten quid that you will become the prime minister one day, whilst they're convinced you're going to become some kind of criminal mastermind. I remember laughing and saying, what's the difference?

I miss your sharp mind and your sharper tongue. There's no one quite like you, Laurel Zanetti. Which is why it's so alarming when you're not yourself. You've been getting quieter and quieter these last few weeks, not really responding to my friendly jibes or the inane things Adeola says. Yesterday, Narumi Hamasaki walked into the common room with some weird 80s hairstyle (no, it was terrible) you would have had a million comments about it but you stayed silent. You've been looking paler than usual and as each day passes you become more and more unresponsive, like reality is becoming a concept you don't quite understand. God, I'm really worried about you, Laurel.

It was only last week that I found out why. Adeola had gone over to your house to check on you and she said your mother looked like she'd been crying, her eyes were red and her cheeks stained with streaking tears. Your father had come down the stairs and told your mother to go rest, whilst he talked to Adeola. He hadn't looked any better, quite ghostly in fact with dark circles under his eyes.

"Laurel doesn't want to see anyone right now," he'd told her.

"Is she alright?" Georgia asked.

Your father had frowned, "She hasn't told you?"

"Told me what?"

Your father sighed and rubbed his eyes, "Luke's been missing for three weeks now."

M.I.A, they call it. Missing in Action. When a soldier is reported missing during wartime.

It had appeared on the news later that evening.

"On March 3rd, 2014, three British soldiers went missing in Afghanistan whilst patrolling in the Kabul District," the reporter wore a solemn face," they were reported missing in the early hours of March 4th and an extensive operation to locate them is underway. Their next of kin were informed within twenty-four hours and are being updated as the operation continues."

They didn't name any of the soldiers but I knew your brother was one of them and everything suddenly clicked into your place. Your silence, your increasing absence from school. I always liked Luke. He's funny and kind even though he's five years older than us, he never treated us like little kids.

I feel so useless right now because I don't know what to say to you. I've experienced loss, the permanent heart wrenching kind but not like yours. Your loss isn't static, it's ever changing, it's a taunting question you can never answer. You must be living in your own version of hell right now, not knowing if your brother is alive or dead, not sure if –

Oh my God. I'm sorry. I'm sorry, Laurel. I'll stop.

You don't need me to remind you of what you're going through. People did that a lot when my mum died, they either offered words of condolences that did nothing for me or they tried to tell me how I felt. "Oh, Morgana, you must be so sad to lose your mother like this." It made me so angry because they couldn't understand how I was feeling. They didn't feel the choking grasp of grief around their necks. They didn't know.

Laurel, you're my friend, and you've always helped whenever I felt lost or unknown. This might not seem like much but I want you to know that I'm here for you. Always, whenever, wherever, I don't mind. Even if it's two a.m. and you can't sleep, I'll stay up with you because I know the nights can be the hardest. When you feel so cold, you can't remember what it was like to be warm.

Laurel, I don't know much about war but I do know a lot about loss. I know that the road is dark right now but the sun always rises. The night doesn't last forever, there is a dawn waiting for you over the horizon, it's going to cast away the cold darkness and greet you with sunlight.

Laurel, please remember, I love you.

And everything's going to be okay. I promise.

Love, Morgana.

CHAPTER 19

N0.19; A LETTER TO SOMEONE YOU JUDGED BY THEIR FIRST IMPRESSION

MARCH 12th, 2014

Dear Imogen,

Pretty, petite Imogen Reed. I remember the first time we met. It was on the first day of Year Seven at Burbank School and the one hundred fifty of us had all been assembled in the Great Hall for induction. Mrs Plummer filed us all in one by one in an orderly line and we filled up the dozen rows of red chairs. I ended up sitting between you and Laurel Zanetti (who would go on to be one of my closest friends at Burbank). We were on the last row and you had scuttled in five minutes late, red faced and sputtering apologies to Mrs Plummer. You slid in the empty chair next to me and offered me an unsure smile. I'd smiled back and you seemed to relax.

Later on that day, you'd bumped into me and sent the stack of folders you held against your chest scattering onto the floor.

"Oh my God...I'm-I'm sorry, s-sorry," you sputtered as you knelt down and began scrambling to pick everything up.

I shook my head and bent down to help you, "It's okay."

When I'd managed to help you collect all your things, you stood up as you sputtered some more apologies. You got all your things and smiled. "Sorry again. I'm such an idiot. I...I was looking for W72 cause I have Spanish and I really don't want to be late."

I agreed to show you to the room since I had French and our classes were across from each other. You'd huffed out this breath of relief and your smile widened into a grin. You reminded me of a pixie, the ones you read about in fairy tales that flew around the forest and got tangled into human affairs. You had a small frame (you still do) and a fair complexion like you hadn't seen much of the sun, your pale blonde hair fell to your elbows and you had these big baby blue eyes. You were so cute and kind but at the same time you were so ditzy and forgetful. You always turned up to lessons late with some excuse about getting lost and you'd trip over your feet when you were talking too much and not looking where you were going.

For about three years, up until Year Ten, you wore a pastel pink ribbon in your hair and you walked around with a lollipop in mouth like you came straight out of a Hello Kitty advert. And for a while (along with everybody) I thought you were the typical dumb blonde. Pretty to look at but nothing going on upstairs. (I'm really sorry for that by the way). But then it all changed about two months into Year Eleven. It was during the weekly assembly for Year Tens and Year Elevens when Mr Weinstein made a surprising announcement.

"This summer, a student from our school had the unique and prestigious honour of being selected to take part of the Inter-national Mathematical Olympiad. A competition that takes the brightest young minds in the world and puts their knowledge to the test," The bored expression he usually wore seemed to melt off for a moment as he continued talking. "This student was only one of six pupils in the country chosen to represent the UK in this challenge."

At this point the entire hall was waiting with baited breath to see who he was talking about. They had to be great if they got Mr Weinstein in a good mood.

"Imogen Reed," Mr Weinstein announced and a chorus of disbelieved murmurs crashed through the hall. "It was Imogen's mathematical know-how that led the team to victory. Imogen, can you please come down here and tell the school about it. It's an amazing feat and I'm sure everybody would love to hear about it."

I remember staring at you with wide eyes as you stood up from your seat and walked over to the front. There was a nervous spring in your step as you climbed up the stairs and onto to the stage. I thought it was some of kind joke because for years you'd be pretty, petite Imogen Reed.

Pretty, petite, Imogen Reed who would forget her own head if it weren't screwed onto her neck. Pretty, petite, Imogen Reed who wore pink lipstick and had the look of a woodland fairy. Pretty, petite Imogen Reed who spoke in a soft, sweetened voice and giggled at the most ridiculous things.

No one would have believed it if Mr Weinstein hadn't shown us the clip of you having to solve a complicated equation involving a "convex quadrilateral" and you having to prove that "line BD was tangent to the circumcircle of triangle TSH" or something like that. It made my head hurt but you solved the entire thing in a little under two minutes without faltering and it was...amazing.

You can imagine my shock when me (and the rest of year found out) you weren't some ditzy blonde but actually the smartest person in our school by a few hundred miles. I mean, you won the UK the most prestigious international academic challenge. I read somewhere the teenagers who took part in the IMO will go on to be some of the greatest mathematical minds of our generation. And you're part of that Imogen. That's...that's amazing.

After that nobody saw you in the same light. I mean, you were still pretty, petite Imogen Reed but you were pretty, petite Imogen Reed with a mind sharper than razor, a mind that could dissect equations faster than a computer and it freaked people out a little. Nobody could believe they'd had you wrong for so long. So many people bombarded you with questions about maths and science and you tried to answer all their questions but I could tell it overwhelmed you.

After that nobody was surprised when you got all A-stars in your GCSEs. It was amazing but it wasn't a surprise. And again nobody was surprised when you picked subjects like Maths, Further Maths, Physics and Philosophy for A Levels. But you did surprise everyone by coming back to Burbank for sixth form, we all thought you would go to a prestigious school like Great Oak Institute. Georgia said it was because you felt more at home here than anywhere else.

You know, you continued to challenge my image of you as pretty, petite Imogen Reed when I found out you were into hard rock bands like Metallica and Muse, certainly not the Spice Girls or Taylor Swift like I'd expected.

We see each other in sixth form a lot and we talk idly, our relationship sits somewhere between acquaintance and friend.

I've always wanted to push it into the realms of friendship but I never knew how. But after today, I think we might be friends. It was fun hanging out with you and Amelia.

At the end of the day, you and I were the only ones left in the computer rooms since we were finishing off our last bit of coursework. I had an essay on the allegorical narrative in Animal Farm for English Lit and you had to document your results for the assessed physics experiment you did the week before. We ended up finishing at the same time and leaving together.

"Don't you usually take the bus?" I asked you as we walked through the school gates.

"Yeah but I'm meeting my girlfriend at Javawocky, it's this nice coffee shop by the high street," you said, "well, she's performing a song and I promised I'd go see her."

I blinked and without thinking I sputtered out, "Wait...Girlfriend?"

Your lips, you'd painted them a deep pink, quirked up into an amused smile as you glanced at me, "Yeah...Amelia, my girlfriend. She goes to Great Oak Institute near the town centre."

"But..." my eyebrows scrunched together, "I thought you were dating Zachariah Baird."

"That was ages ago, like, the beginning of Year Twelve, and it lasted a month tops," you said. "I've been dating Amelia for about eight months now –" you paused, your cheeks turning the same deep pink as your lipstick, "– and she's way better than him. He was a bit of a prick."

I thought about the way he talked down to people and nodded, "Yeah he is."

"You could come with me if you want," you said as we came to a zebra crossing.

"What?"

"Come with me to watch Amelia sing," You said, "she's really good and plus I get extra points for bringing a friend."

I hummed in thought as I pulled out my mobile and checked the time. It had just turned six and the sky was still light.

"Amelia's got a car so she can drop you home," you said and when I turned to look at you, you had a blinding smile on your lips. It made it hard for me to say no.

"Oh, okay," I said, "Sounds good."

Javawocky (I love that name) is a relatively nice café situated between Waterstones and a phone shop. We sat at the front, right near the little stage. You ordered a cappuccino and I ordered some bubble tea (all because Adeola had been nagging me to try it.) In about ten minutes, Amelia came on stage (I knew it was her by the way your blue eyes just seemed to get bluer) with a guitar slung across her chest. She looked older than seventeen, she had a mature air to her like she had just twenty-five and the world had finally started to make sense. She was beautiful with long, honey brown she'd pulled back in a messy bun and sharp grey eyes that kept landing on you every so often. She had a lovely voice, and she sang with a fragile tenderness that captivated the entire shop.

When she'd finish and the final guitar note hung in the air, the coffee shop broke out in a round of applause. Amelia thanked everyone and walked over to us. You stood up as she neared and giggled when she leaned forward and kissed you. She held you like were something precious and my heart ached for a love like that. Both your cheeks were red when you pulled apart.

"Thanks for coming babe," Amelia said to you, her fingers grazing your reddened cheeks.

"Y-you were really good," you replied and then your eyes widened suddenly as you glanced at me, "Oh, oh my God, sorry..." You laughed, "Morgana this is Amelia, Amelia this is Morgana, she goes to my school."

Amelia's hand dropped from your cheek and she turned to me with a sincere smile. "Hi, it's nice meet you."

I smiled back, "You too, y'know you have a lovely voice. Did you write that song? It was amazing."

"Yes I did," Amelia had nodded and grinned, I noticed you watching with the same grin, like sunshine in mid-July, "Thank you! I'm glad you liked it."

You bumped her shoulder, "See, I told you, you were stellar."

Amelia laughed, and pressed a kiss to your cheek, "I know, I know, you're always right." She glanced back at the bar, "Oh wait, I need to talk to the manager about my next performance, I'll be right back."

You watched her go and when she disappeared through the door in the corner, you turned back to me. "C'mon, let's go wait outside," you said, "it's a bit stuffy in here."

We walked out into the street, the sun had gone and the night had taken its place. The air had a chilly bite to it so I stuffed my hands in my jacket pockets.

"Which universities did you apply to?" I asked you as we waited in the spring night. We stood close enough for our shoulders to touch.

"Imperial College London, M.I.T, Cambridge, Tokyo and Stanford," you replied.

My eyebrows rose, "uh...Wow....what are you studying?"

"Aerospace Engineering," you said.

"Wow," I said again, not exactly sure what aerospace engineering was but I knew that if you were doing it had to be hard.

Then again what else did I expect from someone as smart as you? The rumour around school is that you were a prodigal genius and I'm starting to believe it.

"But to be honest, M.I.T and Imperial are the only universities with the kind of aerospace engineering program I'm interested in."

"Aerospace engineering....? Does that have to do with planes?"

"Well, it's concerned with engineering aircraft and spacecraft," you said, your blue eyes finding mine, "but I'm more interested in astronautics...which is basically developing spaceships."

My eyebrows rose once again, "You wanna design spaceships?"

"That and other things but...yeah," you said, "I want to be the one who makes the spaceship for the first manned mission to Mars in the 2030s."

You huffed out a breath and glanced up at the sky. Wonder and reverence painted your features. I watched you, noting the way your blonde hair swirled in the March wind and the rising smile on your face and for probably the millionth time since I'd known you, I noted how small you were. Barely five foot one but you looked at the universe like you were just as grand. And I thought that in another life, in another universe, I could see myself falling for you.

It was hard to tear my eyes away from you but I did to get a glimpse at the stars that had captured your attention. I thought about the first people to arrive on Mars, and the spaceship you would inevitably design to get them there. I thought about how they would be the first people to colonise the infamous red planet, it would usher in a new age of space exploration.

"When they go to Mars," I began, my voice was almost a whisper, "when the spaceship shoots off into the darkness, don't you feel. ..don't you feel like you're being left behind?"

"Not at all," You said, "you're thinking too small, Morgana. You have to look at the bigger picture. You have to think as a species not as an individual, think beyond yourself. As a species, we're going forward."

We were quiet for a long while. Eventually, your blue eyes left the sky and landed on me. "What about you? Which uni are you going to?"

"I've applied to a few but I haven't decided yet," I said, looking back at you. The end of sixth form was approaching and with it came decisions about our future. The future was a foreign land I had no desire to visit but I would have to sooner or later, whether I wanted to or not. "Reading, Leeds, Portsmouth, Liverpool...and...oh yeah Edinburgh."

"To do what?"

"Law."

"Law?" you said, sounding a little surprised.

I didn't tell you about the sudden, crippling urge to help – to make some kind of difference in the world – that had been consuming me these past couple months. It was the reason I'd started volunteering at the local charity shop in centre of town. I've been working there for a little over a month now and since then I've felt another slice of peace slot in my life.

I laughed, "Yeah I know but I want to help people and..." I chuckled, "I was part of the school debate team for a few years in secondary school, so I think I can hold my own up in a court."

"Oh yeah, I remember that," you smiled, "you were really good, I think you won the school a few medals."

The debate team was so geeky but the same time it felt good to take my frustration out on myself in the topical arguments.

"But there's gotta be at least one uni you have your heart set on," you said.

I considered lying but at the last second decided against it. "Edinburgh. It's got one of the best law schools in the UK and it's such a beautiful city, I went there last year to visit some family and I fell in love with it, it's the only place I actually see myself studying," I chuckled, "not to mention I'm obsessed with Scottish accents but...." I shook my head and frowned, "I got in, I mean, I got accepted."

"Isn't that a good thing?"

"They want three A's," I said, "I don't know if I can get that."

"What did you get last year?"

"BBCC," I said, "I dropped Sociology on Results Day, so it's BBC now.

You hummed, lost in your own thoughts for a few seconds. "Then it shouldn't be too hard to get those A's Morgana."

But it would be, I thought, I can't get three A's.

I scuffed my feet on the ground. "Mm. Maybe."

You must have heard the uncertainty in my voice because you sighed and told me to look at you. When I did, I was met with your piercing gaze, your eyes were a bright blue that seemed to burn through the dim light of the spring night.

"Morgana," There was steel in your voice as you spoke. It made my eyes widen just a fraction. "I-I don't get you, which is really frustrating for me because I usually get everything."

I frowned, "I'm not an equation, Imogen."

"Yes but...Morgana, what makes you think you can't get three A's?"

I shrugged. "I don't know."

I really didn't.

"Listen, if you want to get anywhere in life you're gonna have to work hard, and if you want to help people as much as you say you want to then you're gonna have to start by helping yourself," you said, the steely look in your eyes didn't leave. "I know you can get the grades but you're scared that if you actually try you'll come up short but...but you won't know if you don't take the risk."

"But, what...Imogen...what if that happens? What if I do try and I still don't get the grades?"

It would mean I wasn't good enough. It would verify all my fears.

"Then you know you at least tried." You said, "There's no failure in that. There's no failure in trying. I know you're good enough to take the risk, Morgana."

We stared at each other, letting the cars drive by and the stars blink down at us. The silence echoed the same one that followed when James thought he would fail his exams and I'd given him similar advice. Now I knew how he'd felt. You didn't look pretty in the evening light, you looked beautiful. You were a new born star in a landscape of darkness that threatened to swallow me whole.

I swallowed and opened my mouth to say something but then Amelia stepped outside and took your attention. An automatic smile spread across your face as she came to your side.

"Morgana, do you want a lift home?" Amelia asked.

I tore my eyes away from you and nodded rather dumbly. "Yes, that would be great...thank you."

When Amelia dropped me off outside my house, I hopped out of the car and thanked her again. I was walking up to my house when I heard you call my name. I glanced back to see you'd wound down the window and had leaned out.

"Hey Morgana! Don't let anyone ever tell you you're not good enough, not even yourself," you said, "Oh, and do me a favour. Listen to the advice you give others and you won't be okay, you'll be stellar."

You grinned and I could see your blue eyes shining from a distance. I nodded and returned your grin, "Okay!"

You sat back in your seat and gave me a thumbs up. I watched you drive away in the car, even when you disappeared around the corner, I stayed there, staring, for a minute or two. When I finally snapped out of my reverie, I went inside. Your words echoing in my head as I stepped into my bedroom.

I logged into UCAS an hour ago and with a shaky breath, I accepted Edinburgh's offer. Oh my God, Imogen. I've accepted Edinburgh as my first choice for university and it all suddenly feels very real. I have to work hard, I have to live and breathe these exams if I want to get the grades for Edinburgh. It's all or nothing. Like you said, true failure is not trying at all and if I try and fail then I know that I still tried.

I guess the reason I'm writing this letter is to thank you for giving me the courage to take a chance on myself and also because I wanted to apologise for ever thinking you were just some ditzy blonde when you turned out to be so much more than that.

Love, Morgana

CHAPTER 20

N0.20; A LETTER TO THE PERSON YOU WISH YOU COULD BE

MARCH 15th, 2014

Dear Me,

On Saturday I was on the bus going to meet up with Adeola, Georgia and Laurel at the cinemas to see The Grand Budapest Hotel. Georgia's been raving about it for weeks 'cause Wes Anderson is her favourite director and she'd somehow convinced us to go see it with her. I really didn't have anything better to do with my weekends (not that I usually do) and I wouldn't mind spending the afternoon with my friends. Anyway, as I was staring blankly out of the bus window, lost in my own thoughts and not really paying any attention to anything the bus came to halt a few cars behind a traffic light.

My eyes flitted up and landed on an extensive poster of a model plastered across the bus opposite. It was a perfume ad for Vera Wang, in which a beautiful, shimmering woman emerged from a lake of gold. She'd pushed her blond hair back, slick with water and stared at me with hooded eyes, her mouth slightly parted.

Behind her, the sky was black and starless and yet she was bathed in gold light. In bold, italic letters the words, Goddess Rising were written in the black sky above her. She looked like she was made of something ethereal, she didn't belong to this world. She was beautiful with smooth, radiant skin and a slim, curvy body so many women would kill to have and so many men wanted in their partners. She was desire personified.

And suddenly a line from The Merchant of Venice came to mind as I stared back at the woman.

"All that glitters is not gold," I mumbled.

The light turned green, the bus lurched and continued down the road. The woman's hooded eyes followed me, almost leering in her gaze. The bus turned a corner and she was out of view and I let out a breath I hadn't realised I'd been holding.

I couldn't get the woman out of my head for the rest of the day and it got me thinking about the person I wish I could be.

You see, I have this idea of myself. This idealised form I've been looking up to all these years. I like to call her Morgana 2.0. An upgraded version I've been scrambling to reach for so long. Do you want to know what she's like? Morgana 2.0 is taller. Her complexion is clear, blemish free and acne resistant. Her hair falls down to her elbows in glossy waves. Her eyes are bright, sharp and all-seeing. Her teeth are white and straight and her smile is award-winning, it could bring armies to their knees. This Morgana doesn't have a black-hole where her heart should be. Her chest is not empty. Her ribcage is made of steel and it protects the beating heart inside it. It's the kind of heart many would kill to have beating for them.

I envy her to the point my vision is clouded with green rage and I want nothing more than to destroy myself in order to become like her. I compare her to the woman I saw on the advert, that golden goddess, and I understand that neither are real. The person I wish I could be, that idealised version of myself is too...too perfect and perfection is a myth. I keep repeating to myself that to err is human. I realise that the person I kept wishing to be all these years, beautiful, tall, confident, radiant, was what society had nailed into me. So, this letter is not to Morgana 2.0. This letter is more to my future self than anyone else.

The person I wish I could be isn't perfect or radiant or even beautiful. Beauty can only take you so far. The person I wish I could be is happy. Happy and loved and comfortable in my own skin. You might want to be desired or loved or immortal but ultimately, I think what we all want is to be happy. It's the only pursuit I will spend the rest of my life searching for.

Unlike perfection, happiness is not a myth. It's as real as the sensation of sunlight falling through the window and warming my skin. I've felt it. It's my little sister's sweet laughter when Evelyn kisses her cheek. It's James' smile, bright and electric. It's my mother holding me close and singing me to sleep. It's looking up at the night sky, stars blinking in the darkness and understanding you are part of something greater than yourself. It's real and attainable and it's the thing only I want. I want to be happy. Maybe, it's the only thing worth being – worth having in life.

Love, Morgana.

CHAPTER 21

N0.21; A LETTER TO THE PERSON THAT GAVE YOU YOUR FAVOURITE MEMORY

MARCH 19th, 2014

Dear Ariel,

You're still so young, you only turned ten last month. Your innocence is so charming, it makes me ache for my childhood. When the world smelt of wild flowers and the days were long and everything was sunshine. The tragedy of growing up is that your innocence is eroded with each year until you're forced to see the world for what it actually is. Dark and lonely. Dark and lonely and not enough. The world is not enough. Never enough.

Sorry, I think I might be talking about myself there. Ariel, I'll make sure you don't grow up to be a body of walking chaos. There has to be someone in the world who sees its beauty, there has to be a light in the darkness and that's you. Too many cynics spoil the world. You have the remedy to make the world good again. You did that for me once. You made me feel something I had forgotten existed. Ariel, do you remember?

I do. I know the exact date. I know everything about that day. Thursday, August 15th 2013.

It was the day I got my results for my AS Level exams and about a month before I went back to my second and final year in sixth form. I hadn't been able to sleep the night before because of nerves. I only got about four and a half hours of sleep since I woke up at six that morning. I groaned at the prospect of work in an hour (I worked as a receptionist for the local hairdressers) and the exam results. I showered, brushed my teeth and went downstairs to get breakfast. I find some comfort in the fact Evelyn would be getting her results as well that day. Whilst mine were for my first year, Evelyn's would be her final exams that determined if she would get into university. In the past couple of weeks she hadn't shown any sign of worry. She did what she always did, smirked like she could tear you down, go out with her friends and come back late into the night. Like her future wasn't dependent on how well she'd done in her exams.

Burbank School would be open from nine o'clock in the morning to four in the afternoon. I left work at one o'clock and went to meet up with Georgia and Laurel at the off licence on Drummond Road, since we'd agreed to walk to school together and get our results. Laurel was confident that she had at least passed Textiles and Georgia was sure she'd bombed practically every exam. I was as unsure as anyone and I just prayed I got decent enough grades. I never expected anything stellar from myself. Just as we entered the assembly hall, Evelyn bumped past me with a bleak expression.

Adeola had winced and said, "Don't think your sister did too well, M."

I frowned but I didn't say anything. When I finally opened my own envelope, my eyes instantly zeroed in on the grades. I did... Well. Better than I thought. I got Two B's in English Lit and Politics and two C's in Sociology and Biology. I was just chuffed not to have gotten a D in anything. After going bowling with Georgia, Laurel and Adeola to celebrate the end of our first year in sixth form, I walked home with the feeling a great weight had left my shoulders and as happy as I was about my results I knew I would have to work even harder next year if I wanted to get into a good university.

As I had suspected Evelyn hadn't done too well, she'd gotten a mix of C's and D's in final results and Dad had not been happy. Evelyn (and neither were Dad and Jasmin) wasn't too happy to find out she would have to resit the year if she wanted to get into Newcastle. I didn't see her for most of the day, so I assumed she had locked herself in her room.

It was when I'd slipped off my converses and walked into the living room to find you watching Pocahontas (for the millionth time that summer). You wore your vampire costume you'd worn to one of your friends' ninth birthday party the month before. Half your wardrobe is full of costumes, from princesses and devils to cats and mermaids. It's been a growing hobby for you ever since Evelyn and I took you trick or treating when you were six years old. Dad's worried that you might be obsessed with this whole costume thing but I don't think so. It's a creative outlet for you, you have such a big imagination, such a unique way of looking at the world that I think will take you far. Who knows, one day, you might be a big movie star.

When I walked into the living room you looked at me and smiled, your vampire teeth looking a little menacing but adorable at the same time. "Morgana!" you beamed.

I glanced at the TV, where Pocahontas was singing about colours in the wind, "you watching Pocahontas again?"

You nodded, "Yeah! Wanna join?"

I thought about going upstairs, switching on my laptop and pointlessly surfing the internet for a couple hours, and decided against it. Your smile was just too endearing for me to turn down the offer. I nodded and dropped down next to you on the sofa. I grabbed a handful of popcorn from the bowl on your lap and stuffed it into my mouth. I smiled as you rested your head on my shoulder and snuggled into me. I somehow ended up singing along with you to the songs. After it finished, you slid off the sofa and changed the TV onto Channel 4.

"I think Doctor Who's on," you said, "Do you want to watch it?"

I was already comfortable on the sofa so I shrugged, "Go on then."

It was probably a re-run but at this point I didn't care. I liked spending time with you.

You skipped through channels in search of Doctor Who, when you saw a flash of Niall Horan's face on one of the music channels and you squealed. You went back to the channel and started clapping at the sight of One Direction. I'd rolled my eyes and smiled.

The sound of hard drums and heavy guitars filled the living room as you turned up the volume.

You jumped up at the same time Harry Styles started singing. You pointed a finger at me, "Maybe it's the way she walked! Straight into my heart and stole it!"

Your brightness was infectious, I could hardly help the grin that pulled across my face.

"C'mon Morgana!" you laughed as you shook your shoulders, "Through the door and past the guards! Just like she already own it!"

I jumped up and spread my arms, "I said, can you bring it back to me?"

You laughed and wagged your finger, "She said, never in your wildest dreams!"

We threw our arms in the air as we sang along with the band. The drums and the guitars swept in. "And we danced all night to the best song ever! We knew every line, now I can't remember, how it goes but I know that I won't forget her cause we danced all night to the best song ever!"

We shook our hips and clapped our hands to the beat, "I think it went oh-oh-oh, I think it yeah-yeah-yeah, I think it went....Oooo oh! Wooo!"

We sang and danced in the middle of the living room, belting our voices and not caring if anyone heard. Suddenly, I was seven years old again and dancing in the kitchen with Evelyn and Mum was standing by the counter, laughing and laughing and my chest ached because the world felt too far away to be real. When the song ended, the blissful high stayed as we collapsed on the sofa laughing. And when Ellie Goulding came on, music engulfed the room once more, we shot up and kept on dancing.

"And we gonna let it burn, burn, burn!" I sang through my grin.

And after, I'd felt flushed with heat so I'd gone out in the garden and you followed behind. The summer air was cool and heavy with the smell of forget-me-nots (the ones Dad had planted months before) and freshly cut grass. In the excitement we'd forgotten to put on our shoes, so when our bare feet landed on the pebbled pathway that snaked through the garden, we laughed and skipped onto the green lawn. The grass was cool and a little wet from the light showers that morning. We lay down and stared up at the orange sky. Oranges and reds and shades of pink I'd never really seen until then burnt in the evening sky. We lay there for a while, just staring and listening to the soundtrack of the suburbs. I closed my eyes and let a foreign feeling wash over me, it was like floating on a river bank and letting the current take you wherever it wished. It was the feeling of letting go and understanding the grand scheme of the universe. It was only later, as I was lying in bed, falling asleep to the same feeling that I realised it was peace.

"Hey, Morgana," you said, voice as soft as the summer breeze rolling by us.

"Mm?" I said, reluctantly opening my eyes.

You'd raised your hand and pointed to a plane moving in the burning sky.

"Where do you think the people on that plane are going?" you asked.

I was quiet for a beat or two, breathing in the cool air. I smiled. "No idea."

We stayed like that for a while, quiet and content enjoying the summer and each other's company. Jasmin came out later and saw your grass stained costume. She took your hand, fussing about you needing a bath and then telling me dinner was ready if I wanted it.

That night I slept better than I had in forever. I had a long dreamless sleep, with no fear of monsters hiding in the darkness and no thoughts breaking up my slumber.

You don't know this but that day in mid-August, when we danced and laughed and watched the sky swirl in colour, was the best thing that happened to me in a long time. I want to thank you for bringing a slice of peace back into my life, it had been gone for so long it was nothing less than fiction to me. I felt true happiness that day, the blistering, all-consuming kind.

When my nights are darkest I think back to that day, to the rush of peace that washed over me and the bright yellow happiness and the nights suddenly don't seem so dark. I can sleep easier and when I wake up in the morning, the sunlight doesn't blind me like always. It bathes me in warmth and the world is in crystal clear clarity.

Love, Morgana.

CHAPTER 22

N0.22; A LETTER ABOUT SOMETHING YOU'RE AFRAID TO ADMIT

MARCH 28th, 2014

Dear James,

For the last few weeks, I've been going into school early to get some work done in the common room when it's still empty. And plus, I like being by myself in the quiet before rest of the school arrive with all the chaos in tow. Exams are less than two months away and I've been revising for about four hours every night. Georgia thinks I'm neurotic for starting this early but she doesn't just how much work I'll need to get through if I want to get three A's. The prospect of going to Edinburgh and getting to study law is the only thing that's pulling through these last few months of sixth form. Like I told you once, these exams are tough but I'm tougher. I have to repeat it to myself every morning. I don't believe it but if I say it long enough, I just might.

Anyway, yesterday, I walked into the common room with my Politics textbooks clutched against my chest, ready to go over what we'd done last lesson and make some concise notes for the more intense periods of revision in mid-April. I stopped a few feet from the double doors when I spotted you sitting on the long sofas in the far corner. You had a pair of headphones over your head, bobbing your head in that adorable way like you always do, as you read a book. When I walked over to you, I saw it was Catcher in the Rye. I watched you for a second, indulging in the way your long dark lashes fanned across your cheeks and the way you nibbled ever so slightly on your lower lip as you read. Butterflies fluttered in my stomach.

I cleared my throat but you didn't look up, the music must have been playing too loudly. So, I sat down next to you and bumped your shoulder. You jumped, as if only remembering other humans existed, and looked at me. Your eyes – bright green in the morning sunlight that cascaded through the windows – widened.

"Morgana, shit," you said as you pulled off your headphones, "you scared me."

I laughed, "What are you doing here? School doesn't start for another hour."

"I could say the same to you."

I gestured to the Politic textbooks in my lap, "Catching up on some work, I do this every morning, what's your excuse?"

You shrugged, "I like the quiet, gives me time to think."

"Same," I said, I glanced at the book in your hand, "Catcher in the Rye? Is that the one you're doing for your English essay?"

"Yeah, I was struggling to find something and Natalie suggested I read Catcher in the Rye," you said, "I'm only on the fifth chapter but it's pretty good."

My nose scrunched up at the mention of Natalie Huxham. It was stupid. I knew she was a perfectly lovely girl, I'd talked to her plenty of times to notice (much to my dismay) she was a sweetheart and I was already half in love with her myself.

"You and Natalie," I began, trying to sound nonchalant but I got the distinct feeling I was failing. "You two...er...you're cute together."

You frowned, your eyebrows furrowing, "What are you talking about?"

"Natalie, she's pretty..." I forced a laugh, "If you don't ask her out already someone else will, James."

You chuckled, "What? I'm not interested in Natalie like that. She's a good friend." You said, "And anyway, I'm not really looking for a relationship right now, not with exams approaching and not after Leon–"

You froze.

"Leon?" I said. "Who's Leon?"

You rubbed the back of your neck – and I could tell you were deciding whether or not to tell me the truth.

"My ex," you said finally, dropping your hand down into your lap, "We dated for about a year back in Year Eleven. He was...he was great but y'know he hadn't quite accepted he was gay yet so...he didn't want anyone to know about us. I didn't want to be anyone's dirty little secret and I didn't want to push him into coming out so I ended things a few weeks before starting sixth form here. Sorry, I..." you gave me a worried glance, "I...I don't really like to talk about it."

I was quiet for a few seconds as I tried to properly process what I'd just heard. "I...um, no, yeah...um God, James, it's fine." I said and paused again, "So, are you...uh... are you gay?"

"Uh, I don't know, I think I might be pansexual if anything," you replied with a casual uncertainty that brought a sudden, overwhelming wave of affection for you. "A person's gender or sexuality or whatever has never really bothered me. I mean –" you shrugged, "you should love someone for who they are, not what they are."

Another wave of affection, this one deeper and all-consuming washed over me. I almost couldn't breathe. You surprise me, James. Just when I think I have you figured out, when I think I can't possible like you anymore you go and surprise me.

I thought about Imogen Reed, about her brilliant mind and her unwavering belief in me, and that somewhere, in some other life I would have fallen for her too. If you hadn't come in my life James, I think I would pining over Imogen right now.

I glanced at you, and smiled, "You can't help who you love."

You smiled back, "No...No, you can't."

I swallowed. The butterflies in my stomach were spinning faster now.

James, this has to be my fourth letter to you. Out everyone, it's you I keep gravitating towards. I would say I was the moon and you were sun but if you look at the sun for too long it blinds you and if you get too close you'll get burnt. Actually, that last part might not apply to you. No. Wait, it might actually apply to me instead.

I don't want to be close enough to get hurt. There's only so many knives a girl can take to the heart, James. I think the last knife, the one cut that makes me bleed and bleed into death will be yours. I'm scared of that one step, the slip that will pull me into your orbit and I'll be falling into you, burning up with each second, blinded by the sheer brightness of your light.

I'm scared because it's too late. I've slipped and I'm falling and falling and there's no catching me. I think it's too late for all the fear. It's all useless now.

It must have been hard for you to talk about Leon, so I'm going to admit something that scares me.

James, I think I might love you. Not the friendly the kind of love. The kind they write about in novels, the kind that led Paris to steal Helen, the reason the stars keep watching humanity even though we make the same mistakes over and over.

Mr Ekwensi says we're too young to know what love is but he's wrong. That would mean we're too young to know hate and death. But I know death, I've felt its black tendrils snaking around my neck in the middle of the night as I struggle to breathe. I know love, I've felt it when you slip your warm hand in mine to tug me to class. I've felt it in the long stretch of our conversations, in the way light floods into my world the moment I see you, in the way you throw your head back and your laughter shoots straight into my chest.

I know love and I know I love you.

It was inevitable wasn't it? You're inevitable, James. All the roads may not lead to you, but all the roads have you waiting somewhere, smiling your sunshine smile.

Love, Morgana.

CHAPTER 23

N0.23; A LETTER TO SOMEONE YOU WANT TO GIVE A SECOND CHANCE

APRIL 2nd, 2014

Dear Dad,

I found you looking at a picture of Mum today. I imagine if sorrow could manifest into a person, it would be you. You looked like its very definition.

I didn't mean to walk in you, I know it was a private moment, something you only allowed yourself to wallow in once in a blue moon but it was a mistake. I'd been searching for the cheese grater since I wanted to make myself a ham sandwich but it was nowhere to be found. I asked Evelyn if she knew where it was and she said you were the last one to use it. So, that's why I went up to your room.

"Hey, Dad," I began as I walked into your bedroom, "have you seen the cheese grater? I want to -"

I paused at the sight of you sitting stiffly at the edge of the bed, holding a picture in your hands but if it was the look on your face that made me freeze. It was dark and lost like you had stumbled back into a storm you thought had passed long ago. I felt cracks snapping into my heart.

"Dad?" I said it softer this time as I stepped further into your room. I was close enough to see the picture holding your attention. My breath stuttered in my throat when I saw it was a picture of Mum. The wear and tear told me it was an old photograph.

She was in a park with two other women but I knew it was her. I could spot Mum in a sea of a thousand people. She looked younger than I'd ever seen her. Young and enchanting and so much like Evelyn, it was jarring. A picnic basket sat before the three of them. I recognised one of the women as Aunt Mala, Mum's older sister. Aunt Mala lay on her side and gave the camera a shining grin whilst the other woman was content with a simple somewhat timid smile.

Mum sat between them on a large blanket with a can of cider in her hands. Her dark hair wasn't in braids or the long wavy style I was so used to. It was cut short in a sharp pixie bob that made her look like she belonged to a rebel group. Behind her lay the city, tall buildings stretched past the bushes and blossoming trees. She wasn't really looking at the camera, she'd turned slightly to the right and there was the hint of smile on her lips as stared at something in the distance. She was beautiful. The camera had captured her in a moment of perfect youth and I could see why you had fallen so madly in love with her.

"Picnics were her favourite thing to do in summer," you said, your voice suddenly cut through the silence. It made me jolt in surprise. "She dragged me, your aunt and her friend out to the park near the University of Cape Town. She said it was too beautiful of a day to stay inside." You huffed out a laugh, "I was supposed to be getting the food out of the picnic basket but she just looked so...so beautiful, I had to take a picture."

I didn't know what to say for a few moments because you hadn't talked about Mum since the funeral. She remained an unspoken presence in our house for years. Jasmin had felt it when she first arrived and she'd been trying her best to work her through it. I think by now she used to it, used to the everlasting shadow of Mum floating in the background.

"How...how old is she here?" I asked once I'd gotten over my initial surprise.

"Twenty-two," he said, he turned the picture over and read out the date scrawled on the back in black pen. "Thursday, March 31st, 1988." You flipped it back over, your eyes scanned the picture like you were searching for something. "This picture was taken about two years before I proposed to her and five years before Evelyn was born. We'd only been dating for a year and a half but I knew then, just like how I know now, I loved her very much."

You didn't say anything for a while, the both of us just stared at the picture of her, both fascinated and entranced by her.

"I named Evelyn after my grandmother who'd passed way when I was a kid," you said, "Your mother decided on Ariel for your little sister after the aunt who raised her."

Your thumb grazed over Mum's face on the picture.

"Evelyn and Ariel were easy to name but you...you were the hardest," you continued, "Do you know why we named you Morgana?"

I shook my head. I'd never liked my name. It felt too harsh and clunky, it wasn't as pretty as Evelyn and Ariel.

"For nine months neither of us could agree on a name and then, about a week after you were born your mother remembered the myths and legends she used to love as a child. Her favourite were the legends of King Arthur and the Knights of the Round Table. Whilst everyone loved King Arthur, Queen Guinevere, Merlin and the knights, your mother said she always rooted for King Arthur's nemesis and half-sister, Morgan le Fay."

I frowned, "I was named after an evil witch?"

You still didn't look at me as you shook your head. Your eyes were glued to the picture of Mum. "You don't understand," you said, "To your mother, Morgan le Fay was more than that. She was a sister, a mother, a healer, an enchantress. She said the reason Morgan had been presented as an evil witch was because there was nothing men feared more than a powerful woman and Morgan le Fey was that and so much more.   She always used to say Morgan le Fay was a symbol of feminine power, of spiritual transformation."

The corner of your mouth tugged up into a faint smile, "So she named you Morgana as a homage to her favourite literary character. She thought you were going to be powerful and a healer like Morgan in your own right. At first I didn't get it but as grew up I could see what she meant."

You finally looked over at me and I froze.

"Morgana," there was an unmistakable tenor of pride in the way you said my name, "You have an innate kindness, a strong need to help others that many don't have. I think you mistake your kindness for weakness, but it's not, it's your greatest strength and it's gonna take you far." You glanced back at the photograph, unaware of the fact my heart had gone wild in my chest.

"Dad-"

"I hope you can forgive me."

I blinked, "For...for what?"

"For not being there for you when your mother died. I fell apart, so to stop myself from completely unravelling I retreated in on myself. So far deep I couldn't hear anyone, couldn't think about anyone else except your mother," you said, your grip on the photograph seemed to tighten until your knuckles were white.

"When I think back to those months all I remember is darkness and the feeling of being crushed by it. It's just...I loved her so much and when she died it was like everything went with her. Everything. God, this is horrible to say but you and your sisters, you reminded so much of her...I couldn't be around you....I'm sorry..."you shook your head, "I should have been there for you. I shouldn't have left you and your sisters to pick up the pieces by yourself. God. You were only kids. I'm so sorry."

I stared at you with wide eyes, my heart beating faster than before.

"I'm sorry," you whispered.

Your voice snapped me out of my stupor. I lifted my hand and placed it gently on your shoulder. "It's okay, Dad," I told you, "It's okay."

I felt stupid because I couldn't think of anything else to say but then you lifted your own hand and placed it over mine. You took a deep breath, your shoulders relaxing as you exhaled.

"You look tired," I said, "You should get some rest."

You said, "I don't think this is the kind of tired you can sleep off."

Once again, I didn't know what to say. Well, what are you supposed to say to something like that?

"Just...w-won't you at least try?" I asked.

You nodded, almost numbly, after a few seconds. I gave your shoulder one last squeeze before my hand slid off. I turned to leave but at the last second decided to kiss your cheek.

"It really is okay," I said and you glanced at me, that faint smile appearing on your lips but it wasn't the longing one you'd given Mum's picture, this one had hope and contentment. "Dad, you know...you know I love you right?"

You choked out a short, elated laugh. "I do now."

I felt a twinge of sadness for you, for thinking I didn't love you all these years. Is that why you'd distanced yourself from me after Mum's death. You thought I hated you?

"And so does Evelyn and Ariel and Jasmin," I said, "we all love you. Very much."

Your smile became a little brighter, "You're just like your mother, Morgana, you're too good for this world."

"Go to sleep, Dad," I said, smiling, "I'll wake you up when dinner's ready."

You nodded and with one last glance, you opened up the drawer and slipped it inside before shutting it again. I left you to get in bed and walked out of the room. Once I was in the corridor, I slumped against the wall and let out a long sigh. I slid down the wall and landed on the floor with a low thud. I closed my eyes. That conversation had drained me. I felt like I had walked for a thousand days but at the same time, I felt good. Like I'd dropped some baggage along the way and after a little break, I could keep going.

When it was time for dinner and I woke you, you asked me if I could help you fix the car engine after school tomorrow since it was acting up. I'd looked at you in surprise because you usually got one of your friends to help you.

"Yeah, sure," I said and then it was your turn to look surprise, as if you hadn't expected me to say yes.

You smiled pleasantly and nodded before we walked into the kitchen for dinner.

It depresses me that you thought I hated you after all these years. Dad, I want to you know that I love you and although it might not seem like it sometimes, I really do love you. And that for the first time in a long time, I actually feel like your daughter. I'm so glad we're giving each other a second chance. I'm looking forward to helping you fix your car tomorrow, to talking to you under the afternoon sky and over the open trunk of the car.

And if you're still wondering if I could ever forgive you that might be problem, because you are already forgiven.

Love, Morgana.

Chapter 24

N O.24; A LETTER TO SOMEONE WHO DIED

APRIL 5th, 2014

Dear Mum,

This is my second attempt at writing you a letter, I've barely started it and I'm already finding it hard to breathe.

I was talking to Dad a few days ago and -

Shit.

Mum, I love you and I -

Fuck.

I'm sorry for swearing, you always scolded me for even saying hell. It's just -

God, Mum, I'm so sorry.

I'm sorry. Every time I try it's like a black ocean is looming over me, waiting, waiting, always waiting. It wants to drown me, consume me, rip every atom of breath from my lungs until I'm wishing for death. It's like the emptiness sitting in my chest seems heavier somehow, denser and the numbness is crawling all over my body.

Mum, there's so much I want to say to you but - I can't. I think I've kept everything, all the grief and shock and cutting desolation, bottled for so long, it's turned into an unmoveable mountain. My breathing is getting faster now, I can feel myself being transported back to your funeral, to my darkest nights, the days my grief was like steel wrapped around my neck.

I'm sorry. I'm so sorry. God, why is that the only thing I can say to you? What's wrong with me?

I'll try again, Mum. I'll try and try and keep trying because I am going to conquer this. I need to talk to you, Mum, to tell you everything, even if it's in a letter you're never gonna get. I owe you that much.

Love, Morgana

CHAPTER 25

NO.25; A LETTER TO THE LAST PERSON YOU MADE A PINKY PROMISE TO

MAY 23rd, 2014

Dear DC,

It's my birthday today. Eighteen years on Earth. I don't know how to feel about that. I'm officially (in the eyes of the law anyway) an adult. I could buy a house. I could get on a plane and move far, far away. Or I could get a plane and come to you. Would you welcome me with that half-smile you always gave when you saw me in class? Or would your eyebrows furrow in that way when you were trying to remember the answer to a test?

I don't know what I want for my birthday. It's weird. As you get older the things you want can't really be bought with money. When I was eight I wanted a Tamagotchi (because everyone in primary school had one and I didn't like being the only person without one) and now, I would give anything to have my mum back. But nothing in the world can do that. Not even you and your charming smiles, DC.

I'm gonna be eighteen years old at exactly 2:57 a.m. Which is in about an hour and twenty minutes. Normally, I would sleep past it but I decided to stay up this year since it is a monumental age (apparently) and I thought I would kill the wait by writing you a letter.

Okay, if I'm being honest, it's because I want to catch the text message you usually send on the time of my birth. It's always been at exactly 2:57 a.m. since you left for Australia two years ago. I hope you got the text I sent on your birthday, I don't know if you did because you didn't reply. I'm worried you changed your number or just forgot about me but I don't think you did. You promised me you wouldn't. As juvenile as it sounds, you pinky promised DC and as you know, I take pinky promises very seriously.

Y'know, thinking about it, the last pinky promise I made was to you. It must have been three years ago now, when we were in Year Ten. It was sometime in March. Yeah, I remember now. We walked home in the late afternoon, I'd stayed behind after school for the debate club (a club you thought was really lame but you still turned up to see all my debates) and you'd stayed behind because you'd had detention. The third one that week might I add.

The air smelt sweet as we walked through the field of blue and white tulips in the local park. You had your hands in your pockets and you whistled a song I vaguely recognised.

"I had a weird thought last night," I'd said without thinking, "Well...Who's going to remember me when I'm gone?"

You were quiet for a long time and I thought you weren't going to answer but then you opened your mouth. "Your children. Your parents. Your sisters. Your friends...." You paused, "Me."

"You? Yeah, right," I laughed, "DC, you can barely remember what you had for breakfast this morning."

"No, Morgs," you said, glancing at me with a faint frown, your dark brown eyes were swimming with something determined, something fiery and it made me feel a little lightheaded. "I'm serious. I'll remember you. You might not realise this, but you're not the kind of person people easily forget."

I chuckled, "Is that a good thing?"

You smirked in that trademark, cutting way of yours. "Trust me, it's a good thing."

I stared at you, "You're serious? About remembering me?"

I stopped walking and you did too, looking at me with a confused frown. "What?"

You were one of the few people that could see the truth under my self-deprecating humour. People don't really think I'm serious about anything, I tend to make light of things, throw in a joke or two but it's not because I don't take care. I do. I care so much I can't breathe but it's because I don't want to see others sad, Mum always told me laughter was the medicine so I always want to make people laugh. The way I see it, the world is sick and grey and it need remedies and colour to make it better. I think comedy is a great remedy.

You nodded then, your eyes bright with mirth. "I promise I'll remember you, long after we part ways, long after you're dead."

I bit my lip to stop myself from smiling. "Well, I promise I won't forget you either." I lifted my hand and stuck my pinky finger out, "I...I pinky promise I won't forget you."

You glanced at my pinky and rolled your eyes, "C'mon, Morgs... what are we, five?"

"Francis," I said as I huffed out your first name, knowing full well that you hated it when I did that. I wiggled my pinky at you, "Do it. Promise me."

You sighed and pulling your right hand out of your trouser pocket, you hooked your pinky with mine. I grinned.

"I, Morgana Jones, pinky promise to remember you for the rest of my life," I said.

"You're so lame," You rolled your eyes again but you were grinning as well. "Fine. I, Francis Sebastien Dawson, pinky promise to remember you for the rest of my life too, Morgs. Even in the afterlife."

We stood there with our pinky fingers hooked together for a moment before we pulled them apart and let our hands fall to our sides.

I laughed as we continued walking. "Even in the afterlife?" I said, "You always gotta take the extra mile, DC."

You pushed me and I laughed harder.

It's just turned 2:57 a.m. I'm eighteen years old. On this warm May morning in 1996, I was born. God. I'm eighteen, I'm eighteen and I keep glancing at my phone, waiting, waiting -

And you just text me with fifteen seconds to spare before 2:58.

Happy Birthday, Morgs! Welcome to the Legal-ly-An-Adult-But-Not-Really-An-Adult Club! It's kinda lame but the part about being able to drink alcohol (legally) makes it waaaay better x

I took a deep breath and messaged you and you messaged me back and it went like that for a good while.

Me: I'm not interested in the alcohol, DC. And u were drinking alcohol way before u turned eighteen.

You: Yeah but now it's legal, Morgs ;)

Me: Thanks btw

You: For what?

Me: Keeping your promise. Thank you.

You: Could never deny you anything, now could I Morgs?

I got the feeling you wanted to say more, like you were stopping yourself from telling a truth you could no longer deny but I might have imagined it (I do that a lot, warp reality in favour of my own) so I didn't comment on it.

Since it's my eighteenth, I'm going to go the cinemas and then bowling with my friends in afternoon. I've never been big on parties or extravagant get-togethers. In the evening, Dad organised a family dinner at some nice restaurant at the edge of Nottingham. Normally, I would dread family dinners but I'm looking forward to this one. It might actually be fun. But I do wish you were here. I always wish you were but more so on my birthday.

So, here I am, three o'clock in the morning of my eighteenth birthday and I feel...I feel good. It's weird a feeling. I'm not used to it. Maybe it has to do with the fact Laurel laughed for the first time since her brother went missing. Or the fact I'm going to be done with sixth form forever soon and I'll never have to go back to Burbank School ever again (except for my Results Day but then that's it). I don't know, but I know that it's a good thing, and I'm not really going question it.

The only sad thing about turning eighteen is that I can no longer say I'm the Dancing Queen, young and sweet and only seventeen.

Love, Morgana.

CHAPTER 26

N O.26; A LETTER TO THE LAST PERSON THAT MADE YOU LAUGH

MAY 29th, 2014

Dear James,

It's always you isn't it? Like a circle spinning to its beginning, I always come back to you. It's tiring and I don't know if I can do it anymore.

It's weird how a day can begin like any another and end like you never imagined. I mean, one minute you're planning to head home after an intense revision session in the library and sleep forever and the next minute you're running into the boy you love in the middle of the high street. To be honest, you looked as surprised I did. It was just outside Waterstones and you looked vaguely pissed off for a second before you realised it was me.

An easy smile shaped your lips as you said, "Morgana!"

I was a little blindsided by you because you weren't in our usual grey and black sixth form uniform. You wore your army green bomber jacket over a white t-shirt and faded black jeans. I've always liked your style, it's so effortless and you always look like you'd just stepped off a runaway. I stared at you for a few seconds, my heart doing will little flips at just how good you looked.

I blinked, finally pulling myself together, "Oh, J-James, uh...I...uh...Hi..." I'm so eloquent aren't I? It was then that I noticed the SLR camera you had in your hands. I raised an eyebrow, "You taking pictures?"

You'd glanced down at the camera and then back to me, "Oh yeah...I needed to get out of the house, y'know clear my head."

I knew you liked photography, you'd mentioned it every once in a while. About how you liked to walk around town, just snapping up pictures of whatever caught your eye. You'd told me it calmed you down, made you feel a little grounded.

"What about you?" You asked, your green eyes flicking to meet mine, "What are you up to? Why are you lurking around the city centre?"

I chuckled, "Shut up, I'm not lurking. If you must know, James, I've been in the library for about three hours," I said, "I thought I would get some more revision before our English exam on Thursday."

We went on like that idly chatting about our exams, about how Sean Neumann had totally deserved that punch in the face from Evelyn 'cause let's face the guy's an arsehole and then you asked me to join you on your little walk around town.

"It'd be nice to have some company," you'd said, tilting your head a little the side in an adorable manner.

When you're looking at a girl like that James, like she's the only person in this world you could possible want to be with, it makes it really hard for her to say no.

"Yeah, alright," I grinned, "I'll grace you with my presence."

You laughed, "Wow, thank you so much."

Plus, what a better way to get a break from revision than to hang out with you? Brilliant, funny, you who wanted to spend some time with me. I didn't really get it but I wasn't about to look a gift horse in the mouth, so I fell into step beside you.

We walked around town together for the next couple of hours, chatting and laughing and everything just felt so right with you. You snapped pictures of people walking by, of St. Barnabas' Cathedral, of the rose bushes and the café signs.

We were walking past the Theatre Royal Concert Hall and you'd just said something about Christine Wellington's new haircut that had me in tears, I wasn't paying attention to where I was going, which is when my foot caught in the one of the metal tram lanes and I stumbled. I would have fallen flat on my face if you hadn't grabbed a hold of my arm and pulled me up. An immediate wave of heat pumped through me because I'd felt it then, just how strong you are. You pulled my weight up, easy, with one hand and no sign of struggle on your face. It's almost embarrassing how hot I found it.

"Whoa," you'd laughed, "watch where you're going."

I couldn't quite look you in the eye. I felt hot all over. I wanted to reach out and squeeze your bicep, I knew I would feel hard muscle there and it made me flustered. I laughed to hide my nervousness. "You're going to be the death of me, James Baxter."

Your hand left my arm and you placed it on the small of my back to push me along, away from the tram lines and onto the street. You grinned at me, "Maybe, if you weren't so clumsy you'd be alright."

We continued our walk around town, and you continued taking pictures, unaware of the fact I was imagining you without your shirt on. You took me to a bookshop near the cinema, it was small and it smelt like sandalwood and cinnamon. Every inch of the walls were stacked with books from Chaucer to Jung. We were in the back, where the lights was dimmer and the books were older and dustier. I had my back against the bookshelf as I read a page from an anthology of poems. A particular had caught my eye and I couldn't stop re-reading it.

"What have we given? My friend," I murmured to myself, "blood shaking in my heart, the awful daring of a moment's surrender, which an age of prudence can never retract-"

"By this, and this only, we have existed." Your voice cut in, deep and clear. My head snapped up to look at you, startled to find you were closer than before. Close enough that I could count your individual lashes and catch the flecks of gold and brown in your green eyes.

"Great poem isn't it? My grandad's obsessed, he used to read it to me all the time. He told me if I had memorise at least one poem in my life then it had to be that," you said, ever so casually, unaware once again of the devastating effect you had on me. "Do you like him?"

"Who...Who?" I said, sounding like a dumbstruck owl.

You didn't take your eyes off me as you said, "T.S. Eliot...Do you ..."

You seemed to be losing your train of thought as your eyes wandered down to my mouth and I felt like I was a second away from combusting.

"James," I tried to say but it came out as a whisper. I couldn't hear anything except the banging beat of my heart.

"Yes, Morgana?" You whispered back.

You placed your hand against the wall of books behind me and leaned in slowly, so slowly I thought I was going mad. The shop suddenly felt smaller, almost infinitesimal and the aisles narrowed, crowding around us. The world felt like it was closing in on itself. Darkening, collapsing until there was only us.

"James," I said your name again because I didn't have anything else to say. Because I loved the way your name felt in my mouth. Because you were looking at me with such intensity it was hard to think let alone breathe. I let my fingers graze the zipper of your bomber jacket.

I whispered, "James."

You leaned in again, closer and closer and closer until I was sure my heart had stopped beating. You placed two fingers under my chin and tilted my face up. I swallowed and closed my eyes. And then, and then finally, finally I felt the soft pressure of your lips against mine. For a second or two it was just that, it was our lips pressing together, then you tilted your head to the side and parted your mouth and the darkness exploded into colours. Blue. White. Red. Pink. Purple. Orange. Green. Yellow.

It felt like a revelation. A truth like no other and it made me go weak at the knees. I had no idea what was I was doing so I just let you lead, I let myself be carried by the currents. You pressed closer into me, until I could feel the solid weight of your body against mine.

I bet you had chocolate for lunch because I had taste in your mouth, sweet and so sugary I could feel a rush coming on. Heat lapped in waves over me, swooping and crashing as you kissed me. You'd slid your hand up my neck and onto my cheek and I'd fisted my hands into your shirt to stop them from shaking. You kissed me slowly, so slowly it was almost maddening. I felt like a map to a world you ached to explore. Your mouth - God, James - your mouth felt like old songs and gold spilling through me and the sweet air on distant islands and -

You pulled away, panting hard and I let out a small whimper at the loss of your lips. I looked at you and I was met with your wide wander-filled eyes that seemed to mirror mine. I remember staring at you, just staring, entranced by the redness of your mouth, by your flushed cheeks and labouring breaths and marvelling at the fact that I had done that. For once, I had disarmed you. For once, I had the code to unlock you.

I stayed pressed up between you and the bookshelf. I swallowed again.

"Morgana," you said, your voice was hoarse and the sound shot straight through me. You traced my bottom lip with your thumb, "Morgana, I think...I think I-"

"Excuse me!" Someone said and we jumped apart.

You almost stumbled over a small heap of books that sent you crashing onto the floor. I squeaked and you quickly pushed yourself up. The person who'd startled us was the spindly owner of the shop. She had her hands on her hips as she glared at us, "I don't know where you think you are but it's certainly not some dirty club where you can just feel each other up! You take your business elsewhere!"

"Shit, I...I..,"I said. I looked at you, you were busy putting the books you'd knocked over back into a pile. It would have been funny if I wasn't so disoriented. I looked back at the lady and raised my hands apologetically, "Sorry, I'm sorry, we didn't...he didn't mean to. He didn't mean to do that."

You looked up at me then, your eyes widened and there might have been something close to hurt or confusion swimming in your green irises but I looked away before I could properly identify it. I had the sudden urge to leave. To run and run and run. To get away from you because I couldn't handle whatever this was.

"I'm sorry," I said again but I wasn't sure exactly who I was apologising to. I turned and hurried out of the shop, ignoring your shouts for me to come back. As soon as I was outside, I started running.

I don't know long I ran but when I came to a stop in the nearby park, I was breathing hard and fast. I slumped onto the grassy floor. My hand lay over my drumming heart and I stared up at the cloudy May sky, fighting fear and confusion as I tried to make sense of what had just happened.

That was two days ago and I haven't seen you since. You've been trying to contact me but I haven't answered any of you calls or texts. Even if I did, I wouldn't know what to say.

When I think back to the kiss, to the way your mouth felt against mine, I feel this rush of beaming happiness, of sunshine and sugar and then the reality of it sets in and I remember you kissed me. You, James Baxter, the boy I've been pining over for two years now and then fear, cold and jagged, cuts through the rushing thrum of yes, yes, yes. It's terrifying to think that you might...might actually feel the same way about me and it makes me want to run. Run and run and run and run until my legs can't take another step.

I can't do this. I just can't. I'm sorry. I can't be around you. You're too - too much for me right now. I need a break. From you. From this. Fuck. God, from everything. I need space. I need - I need to breathe. But the air has solidified into a weight that crushes me into the ground.

I'm sorry. I thought I was getting better but I'm not am I? I'm still the same hollow thing I've always been. I'm formless. I'm faithless. I'm never fearless. I thought -

I thought I could - I could -

God. I don't know. I don't know anything. I'm sorry, James. I'm sorry.

Love, Morgana.

CHAPTER 27

N O.27; A LETTER ABOUT YOUR THOUGHTS AT THIS MOMENT

JUNE 4th, 2014

Dear Somebody,

It's one in the morning. I can't sleep. And I keep -

I keep thinking -

I keeping thinking that I'm going to die on this planet. On this little clump of rock at the edge of the galaxy, hurtling through the universe. It's a stupid thought because where else am I going to die? But it's also terrifying in this definitive sort of way because my grave is here. It's sitting somewhere on this planet, it's already been written and everything I've done, everything I will do is just a path to my end.

I keep thinking -

I'm never going to see the universe. The different galaxies. The planets. The black-holes. Everything it has to offer. Not in person anyway. I'm always going to be staring up at the stars for the rest of my life. Always looking, never....never actually there, y'know? It makes me want to scream.

Sometimes, I'll lie on my bed just staring up at the ceiling. Most of the times, I'll wish for the ceiling to be ripped off and suck me into space. I'll be dead within a few minutes but at least I got to see the earth in a way only astronauts and satellites have had the privilege. It would be nice to just float in the darkness with the earth spinning below me and suns, old and new, shining and dying all around me.

I told James this once, back in Year Twelve and something flickered in his eyes, like he understood my trembling need to escape but he saw no escape route.

"But Morgana...dying on earth," he'd said, "what's bad about that? It's home. Everything and everyone you've ever known is here. Why would you want to die on some cold distant planet far away from home?"

I think back to that whenever the urge to be swallowed by a black hole rears its ugly head. Home. Home is Nottingham. Home is Sunday dinners with my family. Home is wherever I am loved. That's a nice thought to go to sleep to isn't it? A nice lullaby like the ones our parents sang to us as children. Home. Home is where James kissed me.

God. James.

I keep thinking about James. About the warmth of his mouth. About the strong grip he had on my hips. About the way he tasted like skittles and all the candy I wasn't allowed to eat when I was a kid. It goes without saying really, James is a good kisser. Like, really, really good. God. He was kissing me like - I don't know - like I was a map to a world he needed to explore. Just thinking about it makes my heart want to burst.

I still haven't talked to him since our kiss. He texted me and even rang but I can't bring myself to answer. Every time I try fear seizes me and I run away. I keep running and I don't know how to stop.

It's now half one in the morning and I don't want to think about James. I don't want to write any more love letters to James Baxter. I can't do it anymore. It's too much. He's too much.

Sorry. My thoughts tend to get a little weird when it's this deep into the night. I start to look in on myself and really, that's when everything goes downhill. I better go to bed before my thoughts stop swirling and manifest claws and sharp teeth to rip me apart.

Goodnight.

Love, Morgana.

CHAPTER 28

NO.28; A LETTER TO A FAMOUS PERSON

JUNE 18th, 2014

Dear Amy Winehouse,

Evelyn cried when you died. You're her favourite artist of all time. She has all your songs, she keeps a collection of your CDs on a shelf above her bed. She listens to them when she's going through hard times, like when she broke up with Harvey Willis in the summer of 2011, she had Back to Black on repeat for three days straight. It drove the whole house mad but by the end of it, she bounced back to her old self. You give her the courage and the strength to carry on in a way no one else can. I once thought I didn't have anyone like that. I used to think I was alone in this world and that life was just one big solitary walk but it's not. At least, I don't think it has to be.

You see, I had an interesting conversation with Evelyn a few days ago. Evelyn and I finished our final exam, I had Government and Politics and she had Geography. As soon as we got in the car, and started driving off, she put Valerie on blast.

I wound down the windows and let the cool June wind swoop in.

Evelyn bobbed her head to the song and sang so badly I couldn't help but laugh. "Valerie! Valerie! Valerie!" She grinned, "Did you have to go to jail? Put your house on up for sale, did you get a good law-yer-er-er?"

She had caught the attention of a few people on the street but she didn't care.

"Thank fuck we're done with these exams. Thank fuck I don't have to see or hear Mr Weinstein's whiny voice ever again," She said as you continued to sing on the stereo, "I'm gonna go home and sleep for ten years and then get so smashed at Narumi Hamasaki's party next week I won't remember my own name." The traffic lights had just turn red and Evelyn came to a stop behind a grey Toyota. She glanced at me, "You coming by the way?"

"To what?" I said, "Narumi's party?"

She nodded.

"Uh...I don't think so...Narumi and I don't really talk anymore so, no. It'd be awkward if I just turned up to a party I wasn't even invited to."

"Oh please, Narumi won't care and anyway, if you're with me, she can't say shit. Just come, most of sixth form will be there..." she smirked, "James will be there."

My stomach did little flips, I tried to keep my face as impassive as possible. I swallowed. "So?"

Evelyn rolled her eyes and looked ahead, "Please, Morgana, I know you like him. You were all buddy, buddy, smoochy, smoochy, a few weeks ago...and now it's just – I don't even know. You've been all quiet and don't think I didn't see the way you and James looked at each other in the library this morning. I ran into his older brother yesterday and he says he's been walking around the house looking like a kicked puppy. And you...you've been all quiet and avoiding school." Her eyes flicked over to me, "What the hell happened?"

I bit the inside of my cheek as my mind travelled back to that late May in the bookshop. I wanted to tell her that I'd run away like a coward after he'd kissed me. I wanted to tell her I'd been ignoring his calls and texts and that I didn't have the courage to just face what had happened and talk to him.

"It's....complicated," I said.

"No, it's not," she said and I looked at her, surprised to find her eyes were already trained on me. "Life isn't complicated, Morgana. It's pretty fucking simple. People just like to say it's complicated so they can either justify their crappy decisions or run away from them. Now, don't bullshit me, do you like him?"

I opened my mouth to say no but I snapped it shut and sighed. I said. "Yeah."

"Does he like you?"

My pulse picked up as I thought back to the way he had kissed me in the bookshop, to the look of wonder on his face like he could hardly believe his eyes and I swallowed. I nodded again, "I...I think so."

And you know what? The world didn't shatter like I thought it would. Finally admitting that James Baxter might actually feel the same way about me was terrifying but liberating all at the same time. I felt like a weight had been lifted off my chest and I could finally breathe.

Evelyn's perfectly made up eyebrows pulled together in confusion as she stared at me. "Then what the fuck are you waiting for?"

I opened my mouth but nothing came out. I didn't have an answer for her. She was right after all, what was I waiting for? I glanced out the window at the afternoon street, watching people walk by and I wandered just how many of them were waiting, if they had fought for what they wanted or let it slip away out of some misplaced sense of pride or self-pity.

And suddenly, I had a vision of myself. Twenty years in the future and I was one of those people, walking down the street with a vacant look on my face and a chasm of deep regret sitting in my chest. Stuck in the days that had gone, living in the ifs and maybes of my life and always wondering what could have been.

And it was petrifying. Ice cold fear splashed over me in great waves and yanked me out of my own self-pitying ignorance. I knew what I had to do, if I wanted to avoid a life of hopeless wishing, I had to stop waiting. I had to stop running.

I looked over at Evelyn with widened eyes and a sudden, if not foreign burst of confidence.

"Take me back to school."

She pondered for a moment, "Hm...nah."

My heart dropped. "Evelyn!"

She laughed. "I'm joking! You should have seen your face," she said grinning, "So, you finally got some balls huh?"

I exhaled, and chuckled, "Something like that."

I'd seen James in the library with Kyle Witter and Clementine Godford, revising for the chemistry exam they had later on that afternoon. I'd turned and walked off as soon as James lifted his head and spotted me staring at him from across the room. I was such an idiot.

Evelyn reached the school gates about fifteen minutes later. I quickly hopped out of the car and slammed the door shut behind me. Evelyn laughed as I started running into the school, my heart pounding in my chest.

"Slap his arse for me!" she shouted from the car and got a few startled looks from the students.

It was time to stop running away from my problems and face them head on. If something broke you fixed it, you didn't leave it and hope it would magically repair itself. If you wanted something you went for it. And all I wanted right then was James Baxter. Evelyn had been right, what was I waiting for? Nothing. There was nothing to fear and everything to take.

I glanced at my phone. It was nearly two o'clock and James had his chemistry exam in exactly fifteen minutes. I needed to talk to him beforehand. I turned a corner, and nearly crashed into a year seven girl. I prayed that he would still be in the library with Kyle and Clementine.

I pushed the double doors open and burst into the library with ragged breaths. God, I was so unfit. I needed to start exercising. My heart lifted when I saw the familiar mop of brown hair. I walked over to him, heart still pounding, and not caring the slightest that people were staring.

Kyle said something but I didn't hear, the blood roaring past my ears was too loud. I cleared my throat and James glanced up. Olive green eyes met mine and for a moment I was lost for words. I stood there like an idiot for several moments as I tried to remember what I wanted to say.

James pursed his mouth, "Morgana?"

"I need to talk to you," I blurted out and I winced at how dumb I sounded. I made a mental note to kick myself later.

Kyle frowned and he said something else but again I didn't hear. It must have his usual arsehole lines because Clementine punched his shoulder and his mouth stopped moving.

"Please," I said, "two minutes that's it."

James stared at me and time seemed to slow down, each second stretching by with a length of ten years and I could feel my rising panic. I thought he wouldn't answer or worse laugh in my face and flip me off. His eyes flicked to Kyle and Clementine for a second before they went back to me. He gave me a short, curt nod and stood up. I tried very hard not to smile as James followed me out of the library and into a small classroom down the hall.

I shut down the door and turned to look at him. Evelyn had been right (again), he did look tired, like he hadn't slept properly in a while and I got the faint feeling that had something to do with me. His chocolate brown hair was mess, sticking out at all angles and he wore his tie loosely around his neck. He wasn't quite looking at me, his gaze directed at a particular spot behind me as he stood with his hands in his pockets. I bit my lip.

"Spit it out, Morgana," he said and glanced at a large map of English rivers to the right. "I have an exam in ten minutes."

This was it. I thought. All or nothing. The pressure was building up in my chest. I didn't know what to say so I just blurted out the first thing that came to mind.

"T.S Eliot," I said and I felt like an idiot. I wouldn't be surprised if he'd walked out right then.

"What?" His eyes finally left the poster and landed on me.

"In the bookshop," I said, feeling my face heat up, "you asked if I liked him – T.S. Eliot, I mean, and yeah, I do like him."

His eyes narrowed, "is this why you came here? To talk about T.S Eliot."

"No! I just...shit," I ran a hand down my face and sighed. I took a deep breath to calm myself down because I was close to exploding. "I wanted...I want to say...I...I'm sorry okay?" I grunted, suddenly so annoyed at myself because I wasn't saying it right. "I'm sorry for running off like that. I just...you were looking at me like –like I was this masterpiece and it scared the shit out of me." The words were coming out jumbled, a mangled mesh that only seemed to become chaotic with each second. "Fuck, look, I'm sorry. I'm not good at...at talking about my feelings let alone dealing with them. And I needed time to think, to sort my head out and when you're around I find it hard to think straight. And...and..." I exhaled, "and...that's it, really."

God. That was so terrible. I must have sounded so lame, I wanted to kick myself again.

I had more to say but a novel's worth of words were still lodged in my throat. Even now, as I write this letter, I can't seem to dislodge them and tell you exactly how I feel. But I think with time, I can. I can give you that James.

I don't know how, but I somehow got the courage to look up and my breath hitched in my throat. There was a deep blush along his cheeks and his lips were parted, like he'd been meaning to say something throughout my meandering speech but I kept cutting him off. He looked just as flustered as I felt.

"I'm sorry," I said again.

"Morgana, you don't have to apologise," he said, looking at me with an unreadable expression, "There's nothing to forgive."

"Oh."

After a long pause, he said, "Have you...um...finished thinking? Did you sort your head out?"

"Yeah," I breathed.

James took a step towards me, his eyes never leaving mine. "And?"

"And I...I..." I grit my teeth and pushed past my nerves, "I really like you, so...yeah."

And he grinned, and oh Amy, he grinned in this bright, blinding way I'd only seen on supernovas and my heart actually stopped beating for a moment. He was the most exquisite thing I'd ever seen.

"Good," he said and his grin was so infectious I couldn't help grinning too. Butterflies swooped in my stomach as my pulse picked up. "Cause, I really like you too, Morgana."

The whole thing felt too surreal and I made a note to pinch myself later.

"Y'know, all week I've been scared shitless I was going to fail this exam but..." he stepped closer until we were only inches apart. "But now you're here, I feel good. You're all the good luck I need."

I was grinning so hard my cheeks were beginning to hurt. "Oh, um, good. I'm glad."

Silence settled over us like a warm blanket for a long moment before it was pierced by a shrilling ring.

We jumped apart. I looked around, scared we'd somehow set the fire alarm off but then I saw him pull his mobile out of his pocket. He chuckled and showed me a picture of Kyle lighting up his screen as his phone rang.

"It's just Kyle," he said, ending the call, "It must be about the exam, it's in five minutes. Shit. I need to go."

I fought down a wave of disappointment and smiled at him. "Oh right, go on then." I said, "Good luck."

He glanced up at me and returned my smile, his was even softer.

And as we looked at each other with soft, bright-eyed faces, a line from the Waste Land came to mind. By this, and this only, we have existed.

"I have to go, I can't miss this exam," he said and headed for the door. When he grabbed the handle, he paused and glanced back at me, "By the way, the exam's like two hours long so I wouldn't wait up."

I laughed, "I wasn't going to but it's nice to see your ego's having a good trip."

"Shut up," He chuckled, "Listen, I'm going to the pub with Imogen, Kyle, Laurel, Seb and Zeke. I think a few others are joining us but I can't remember who." He licked his lips, "You'll come?"

My eyebrows had almost shot up at the mention of Laurel coming out. Since her brother's death, she'd been almost ghostly in her silence but lately been speaking more, choosing to join in the conversations and even make one of her classic quips. I hadn't thought she'd be ready to go out for another month or so but just the prospect of seeing her had lifted up my mood tenfold.

I smiled as I clasped my hands together and nodded. "I'll be there. I promise."

"Great," He grinned in a disarming way that had the laughter dying in my throat. "I'll pick you up at around seven?"

"Seven's good," I said, nodding once more.

God, you should have seen him Amy. He reminded me of poetry.

He was gorgeous, a blinding supernova in the bleak cosmos.

And as I watched him go, I thought –

I thought, love is a terror but it's the only terror worth enduring.

Love, Morgana.

CHAPTER 29

Dear Mum,

I'm so sorry it's taken me so long to write you a letter, well, a proper letter that didn't start or end with me crying.

It's been so long since we last spoke. Eight years and fifteen days to be exact. I remember the last thing you said to me. Do you? You were lying in your hospital bed as you had been for the last year and I was crying because you looked so pale and deathly.

You'd taken my hand and said, "I promise you everything's going to be okay, all you have to do is have a little courage."

I'd stared at you with tears in my eyes, "I don't have courage."

"Morgana," you said, giving my hand a squeeze. "True courage isn't built in an instant."

I never quite understood what you meant but it'd somehow made me feel better. I've been puzzling over it for years. But I think I get it now. True courage isn't built in an instant because it takes something more than a split decision. I think that's the difference between bravery and courage, bravery is done by ignoring or lacking fear in that very moment. Courage is something deeper, more profound. It comes from the heart, from recognising the horror of your situation and despite your own fear, you push forward and resolve to do it anyway.

And I feel as if I've finally built up the courage to put down this pen and tell you everything I should have said all those years ago.

Mum. I love you and I miss you. I love you so much and I miss you every single day. When you died the whole world seemed to fall away and for a while, nothing else mattered, not really, not if you weren't there. The world lost its colour and I remember living in cold greyscale.

Dad locked himself away in your bedroom for months, he was static, I was so scared I was going to lose him too. Aunt Mala took care of us in those months. She kept telling us everything was going to be okay, and looking back, I think she was trying to convince herself. Evelyn and I argued a lot, and I mean a lot. I don't think I hated anyone as much as I hated Evelyn in the two years following your death. After that the hatred cooled down to cold indifference. Ariel was too young to understand any of it so she cried and kept the whole house awake.

Once the shock fell away, it gave way to numbness and then a heavy, crushing weight on my chest. It made it difficult to breathe. When night came, the weight became heavier and I thought I would die from the pain, some nights I wished I would. In those first six months it felt like the devil was ripping through my veins and unleashing hell in every corner of my life. Nothing can prepare for death. Not your own, or death of the ones you love.

Eight years later and it still hurts but not as much. Some days, I'll see the same grief reflected in Dad and Evelyn's eyes and I feel so furious, so suddenly furious at the world, at God for taking you away from us. Some days, I'll be okay, I'll be laughing with my friends or watching the television but then something reminds me of you and my heart feels too heavy to carry in my chest. Some days, a wave will hit me. It's black and so freezing it leaves me dizzy and breathless. And then it'll pass and just like that I'm breathing and walking again and the world doesn't seem so dark.

The world isn't dark, not really. A lot's happened since you died. Ariel was a baby when you last saw her, she's ten years old now and she has a startling resemblance to Aunt Mala when she was a kid. Oh, I wish you'd seen her grow up. She's amazing. She's the first bar of sunlight in the aftermath of a stormy night. She's growing so fast, she's already in her last year of primary school and next year, she'll be in secondary school.

She wants to go to Burbank like Evelyn and I but I hated Burbank, so I'm trying to convince Dad and Jasmin to let her go to Great Oaks Institute or even St. Sebastien's. They're much better schools. She's angling towards St. Sebastien's since it's an all-girls school and she thinks boys are so "yucky". She says five years without them would be a blessing.

Evelyn is nineteen and out of the three of us, she looks the most like you. Everyone always tells her this but she keeps saying that she doesn't see it. She's very beautiful now, and she has all these boys (and even some girls) wrapped around her little finger. You always said Evelyn was the energy that drove a party and you weren't wrong. Evelyn and I aren't best friends like we used to be, but we are on good terms. It's so much easier to talk to her now, we even laugh and joke. I might even say we're friends. Well, nearly. Give it a bit longer. The years of resentment between us need time to bleed out.

Dad loves you very much, and I think your death hit him the hardest. He wasn't himself for a while after you died, he wasn't anything really. He just lay in bed, curled up under the covers and listening to your old records. It took almost two years to guide him out of the darkness, and even though he has his moments, he's okay. He's gotten a lot better since he met Jasmin. I don't think I've told you about her. They met about three years after you died, it was at a bereavement group Aunt Mala had convinced Dad to go to because if he couldn't talk to her (I think it's because she reminded him of you) then he would have to talk to somebody.

Jasmin had been in the same support group as him. She'd lost her father a few months back. They didn't say much in the groups but they said a lot to each other, I think they helped one another through the grief. One day, Dad asked Jasmin out to coffee and then one thing led to another two years later they were married. I didn't like her at first, I thought she was replacing you but then Ariel pointed out just how happy she made Dad. I hadn't seen him smile like that in a long time and if Jasmin was responsible for bringing some joy back into his life then I couldn't really hate her. Dad still loves you of course, I think he always will.

And me? Well, I'm eighteen now and I'm...I'm good. It feels great to actually say that and mean it this time. I finished sixth form in June and then in August we got our exam results. I hadn't realised how much I wanted it until I was holding the envelope in my hands. My heart pounded as I pulled the letter out. My jaw actually dropped, Mum.

Two A's in Politics and Biology and an A-star in English Literature. Can you believe that? I must have stared at the letter for five minutes, my heart still pounding, not believing what I saw. Jesus Christ. Two A's and an A star, Mum, I nearly cried. All those long days and nights spent in the library, surrounded by nothing but books and endless notebooks, were worth it. I'd been so scared, so powered by the prospect of failure and the need to prove to myself that I could actually do this. And I did, Mum. I did it! I did it!

Imogen Reed had hugged me and said, "See! I knew you were good enough! I told you could it!"

I'd grinned at her and glanced back dazedly at my results.

James had walked over to me then, holding his own envelope in his hands and pressed a soft kiss to my forehead. "Congrats, Morgana."

I smiled, "Thank you! How about you? How did you do?"

He waved the letter, his grin seemed to brighten and I found it difficult to breathe and it wasn't because of my results.

"B in English Lit, A in Biology and an A in Maths," he said, "I got into Manchester!"

My eyes widened and I leaped forward to wrap my arms around him. I grinned into his neck. "That's amazing!"

He hugged me back and laughed, the sound vibrating in my chest.

Oh, Mum, I met a boy (isn't that how all those great tragedies begin? I hope ours doesn't end like that) and his name is James Baxter. Oh, Mum, have I told you about him? He's wonderful. He's a star. I think you would like him, I mean, he thinks the Beatles are the best thing since slice bread so you two would definitely be best friends or something.

It was only until Georgia and Adeola were congratulating each other for getting into university that I realised I'd gotten into Edinburgh. I had to fight back the tears. I was so happy I'd run over to them and pulled the both of them into hugs. Victory was a foreign emotion but it was welcomed. I'd looked over at Evelyn to find she was celebrating too. Turns out she got two B's and an A, which is what she needed to get into Newcastle to study Geography. She'd grinned at me from across the room and I'd returned her glee with the same grin and two thumbs up. Dad had never looked so proud when we came that day, he'd said the both of us and said you'd be just as proud of us, of your little girls all grown up and going to university. Evelyn had made some excuse about needing the toilet but I could tell she was fighting back tears just like me.

I'm writing this letter in my bedroom on the desk near my window. It's two in the afternoon and it's raining outside. I'm going to university tomorrow. As you know Edinburgh is a long way from Nottingham, almost three hundred miles, so Dad booked a flight there since the train ride would be too long. On the plane it's only an hour, and since he's working tomorrow, Jasmin is accompanying me on the flight. Which I don't mind, I like talking to her. Dad's driving Jas and I to the airport tomorrow afternoon to catch the flight for two o'clock. James text me earlier, saying that he was coming with me to the airport to say goodbye. He won't be leaving for Manchester until next Saturday, so we're both feeling pretty emotional about my departure. I don't know how I'm going to say goodbye to him. I think I might be crying too much to even say it to be honest. It's silly, I mean, it's not really goodbye because I'm going to see him again at Christmas or even before that. We promised each other we would visit one another at university at least once in the first term. And like always, I plan to keep my promise.

You know, I still can't believe James Baxter is my boyfriend, I have to pinch myself every once in a while to check if I'm dreaming.

James and I have been dating for about two months now. (I accidently called him my boyfriend back in early June when we were watching a movie at his, and both our eyes had widened. I thought he was going to run away but to my pleasant surprise, he'd just grinned and made out with me for a while.) We had a long talk about us a few nights ago, a talk we'd both been dreading. We're both going to separate universities (along with our friends), he's off to study Economics at Manchester and I'll be studying Law all the way in Edinburgh.

We'd considered the option of breaking things off but neither of us could bear the thought so we agreed to stay together. I don't want to lose James when I just got him. A long distance relationship is going to be hard but he's worth it. If things don't work out then at least we know we tried. I have a lot of faith in us. I know we can do it, because I love him and he- and he loves me too.

University is scary but it's new and exciting and I can't wait to begin. The future looks bold and bright. I want to get my law degree and make you and Dad so proud of me. But most of all, I want to do it for myself.

Mum, you left too soon but I know you're at peace. And I feel a similar calm washing over me as I write this. It settles in my chest and floods into every vacant chasm in my body. I don't feel as lost, if anything, I feel found. And I know that whatever happens, good or bad, you'll always be watching over me.

Oh, one last thing before I go.

I miss you, Mum, and I will always love you.

Love, Morgana.

Epilogue

N O.30; A LETTER TO ANYONE WHO FEELS LOST AND UN-KNOWN

DECEMBER 31st, 2014

Dear Somebody,

It's New Year's Eve and Jasmin has been running around all day trying to get everything ready for the big dinner tonight. Her parents are coming and so are some of our cousins from London and Cape Town. She's letting Evelyn and I invite a friend, so Evelyn is bringing Octavia Cross, one of her best mates from university who coincidentally also lives in Nottingham. So, I'm inviting James over. The dinner starts in an hour and he said he would be here about thirty minutes beforehand so we could "chill" but I have a feeling we're just going to end up kissing on my bed (not that I'm complaining). I don't have much time and Jasmin is already calling my name to help set the table but I really needed to get this off my chest.

These days, I look in the mirror and I don't see the face of the enemy. All I see is a girl who's just trying to figure everything out, step by step, day by day, taking the future as it comes.

And yes, I don't know what the future holds and that used to bring an onset of panic like a claw ripping into my chest but now, now the obscurity of the future is almost comforting. To know whatever happens or may not happen is mine to set in stone. I may not know my place in the grand scheme of the universe but I know it still is a place, however or small or great, we all have our roles to play.

And I know I'm going to have dark days and I know I'm going to make mistakes along the way and that's okay. It's okay as long as I remember to pick myself up each time and keep going because life is a long, winding road but it's not a road you have to walk alone. Help is always at hand for those who need it and it might be scary, but all you have to do is ask.

You know, Maya Angelou is my favourite author in the world and she once said something that's been in my playing in my head for weeks and months and years.

You alone are enough. You have nothing to prove to anybody.

I never truly understood it until now. Each word is a different kind of confession and I repeat it to myself. I repeat it over and over.

You alone are enough. You have nothing to prove to anybody.

There's freedom in that, it's a brand of freedom no one else can give you. It's a brand of freedom you can only give yourself. A self-liberation that shakes you to the core. I repeat it until it's the only thing I know, until it's infused in my very being.

I am enough. I have nothing to prove to anybody.

And for the first time in a long, long, long time, I can say this. I'm going to be okay.

If you're reading this, you're going to be okay too.

Love, Morgana.